Dress You Up

Dress

A Capsule Collection of
Fashionable Fiction

EDITED BY
BRIAN
CENTRONE

You Up

Dress You Up:
A Capsule Collection of Fashionable Fiction

Published by New Lit Salon Press, 2021

© 2021 New Lit Salon Press, LLC

Edited by Brian Centrone
Line and Copy Edited by Helen Evrard
Illustrations by Stephen Tornero
Art Direction by Brian Centrone
Design by luke kurtis

"This One's Not for Us" was originally published as "Life Will Be Better" by *DNA*. It was runner up for their OUT OF PRINT Short Fiction Contest, which was published at dnaindia.com on 22 November 2015.

New Lit Salon Press
Carmel, NY

Print ISBN 978-0-9972649-3-7

www.newlitsalonpress.com

Contents

"A Pocket for Secrets" by Susan Carey • 7

"This One's Not for Us" by Farah Ahamed • 16

"A Statement Bag" by Gerri Leen • 25

"A Weekend with Imogen" by Cheney Luttich • 30

"Battle Jacket" by Blake Jessop • 42

"42nd Street Shuttle" by Linda Welters • 54

"The Weight of a Bag" by Gabriella Brand • 58

"Hemlines" by P.J. Schaefer • 69

"Second Hand Rose" by Lindsay Bamfield • 78

"A Significant Other" by Larissa Hikel • 83

"The Wedding Dress" by Evelyn Forest • 89

"It Matches Your Eyes" by Madeleine McDonald • 94

Contributors • 102

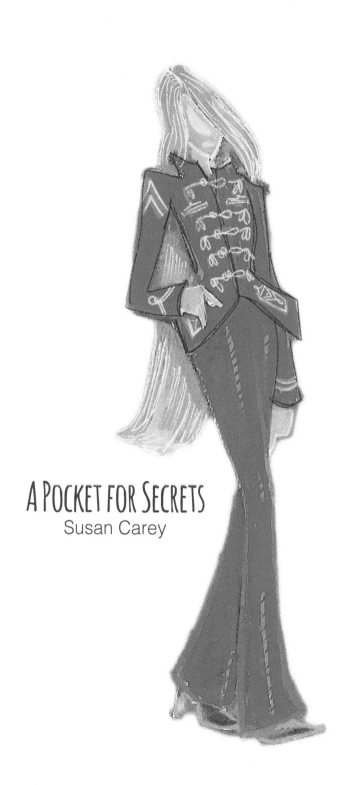

A Pocket for Secrets

Susan Carey

The shop window sits like a squashed child between elegant gabled houses along a dark street in Amsterdam. Inside is a jeweled grotto of color, pattern and texture. I know the owner—Annie Holtman—well, and we often pore over the latest fabrics. On this day Annie is putting a bolt of rainbow-striped chiffon on the shelf. She eases the new cloth between bolts of tie-dyed cotton and purple corduroy in the flower-power corner. The clash of colors is dizzying. Two young women enter the shop in diaphanous skirts and cowboy boots. Like bees to a flower, they head straight for the new fabric, leaving a trail of patchouli scent as they pass.

In the silk and velvet section, the shades are so vivid you can picture gamine ladies in evening gowns and hear the clinking of champagne flutes and the swish of hems on marbled floors. My fingers are drawn to a flash-of-kingfisher blue velvet, and I sigh softly. I will never sew again, you see, and only Annie understands why. Yes, my fingers are slightly arthritic, and my eyesight not so good, but these are not the reasons.

Despite this, I keep my home machine in good condition. Now that Lenny is dead, there is only me to lift the heavy sewing machine out of its cubbyhole. The noise of oil lubricating its moving parts takes me right back. Even when the trees are bare, the sound never fails to break me out in a sweat.

Jocelyn, my granddaughter, has just turned twenty, and she will soon graduate from the Rietveld Academy, where she studies art. Years ago, I was the best seamstress on the Waterlooplein, and last week Jocelyn brought me a pattern for a velvet trouser suit. She had seen a similar outfit—by some fancy designer I've never heard of—and said, "Please, *Oma*, I know you can sew, even though you might be a bit rusty. I want to wear something fab and unique for my special day."

She knows her own mind, I have to give her that. The trousers have flares that young people wear nowadays. The jacket, tailored at the waist, flows into a peplum. It has a mandarin collar, and closures of silver-braid frogging that loop over toggles.

The velvet in the shop exactly matches the hue of the blue scarf worn by "The Girl with the Pearl Earring." A copy of the painting hangs in my hallway and is the first thing I see when I get home. I gaze at the picture, thinking the color would look perfect against my granddaughter's hair, which glows like golden ripe barley. The ghost of the velvet nap still purrs beneath my fingers, so different from the knife-like linen I used to sew that felt as cruel as a winter's day.

A tap at the window makes me turn around to find Jocelyn waving as she holds up a paper bag. Her smile could thaw a frozen canal. She ushers in cold air as Kwibus, my cat, rubs against her legs in delight.

"I was just thinking of you," I say, and—after switching on the percolator—take out two china plates and dainty forks almost small enough for a doll's house.

Jocelyn divides the *poffertjes* on the two plates. "They're still warm, I just bought them at the market." We sit down in the living room, and Jocelyn tries to stab a mini pancake with her fork.

"Oma, I'm going to use my fingers, this fork is too fiddly."

"Is that oil paint on your hands? Here's a napkin, dear."

"Just been finishing one of the last pictures for my studio show."

Icing sugar sticks to her fingers. Kwibus jumps on her lap and meows, and Jocelyn lets him lick her fingers clean. She nods towards the unopened sewing pattern which rests against a vase of tulips on the table and says, "It's only a few weeks now till graduation day."

"Mmm," I say, dabbing my lips with my own napkin.

"How long will it take to make the suit? Do you need to measure me?"

"I've got your measurements, don't worry. And remember to get your nails done in time." I nod toward her paint-splattered fingers. "A woman's hands should never let her down."

The next morning, the clamor of the barrow boys setting up the market around the Westerkerk awakens me. I dress quickly and go out the door. Tall houses reflected in the canal waltz and glisten like shy lovers.

Annie's eyes pop out on stalks when I say I want five meters of the kingfisher velvet. The fabric shimmers in her hand when she cuts as the scissors make that satisfying *scree scree* sound like seagulls that arc, so high and free, above the canals. As I leave the shop, Annie hands me an envelope with my name, Sarah Jacobs, hand-written on the front. "From a friend."

I raise my eyebrows and ask, "*What* friend?"

"Someone from the *old days*."

The envelope smells faintly of rose scent, and I tuck it in my pocket for later.

Once home, I tear off my coat and toss it over a chair in the hallway. Just the thought of sewing again sets my insides roiling, and I rush to the lavatory. My stomach is empty, so I can only dry retch. Stirring up all those old memories is a damn fool idea Lenny would have said. But how can I take the fabric back? Even though Annie gave me a discount, it was still eye-wateringly expensive.

Lenny's cure-all may help my nausea: a shot of Dutch gin poured so generously that it almost spills over the rim of the fluted glass. I sit down at the dining table, watch the flower seller extending the awning to shelter from a downpour, and knock the drink back in one swallow. The burn gives me courage, and I am ready to meet my nemesis. First, I lay the fabric on the table, ready for cutting. The rain suddenly stops, and the sun comes out. Reflections from the canal cast rippling slivers of light on the walls and surfaces. The velvet ebbs and flows, an ocean with its own opaque, silent depths.

The pattern pieces are slippery between my fingers, and the numbers, arrows, darts and dots blur in front of my eyes so that I lose balance and have to grip the table's edge. I put on my glasses and open my sewing box. The smell of tailor's chalk triggers the nausea again. I slam the box shut. It's not too late. I can still change my mind; the fabric isn't cut yet.

"Holtman Fabric and Haberdashery. Mrs. Holtman speaking."

"Annie, it's me, Sarah. Trying to sew again was a silly idea. Can I bring the velvet back and do some hours in the shop to compensate? Isn't it time for your yearly pilgrimage? I'll cover for you."

"I went last month. That's when I was given the letter. You know, the one I passed on to you."

My coat still lies draped over the chair; the letter forgotten in its pocket.

"Just bring the fabric back, Sarah, and it will go in the remnants pile. Why do something that makes you feel bad?" She takes a deep breath. "What's a few meters of cloth between friends?"

"Thank you, Annie. Thank you." The telephone receiver clicks.

I fold the fabric up and slide it back into the paper bag, then put it in the cubbyhole on top of the sewing machine. I'm sure that I can find an off-the-peg outfit for my granddaughter in the Bijenkorf, the big department store on Dam Square.

Back from my shopping expedition, I sit down to enjoy the only thing I bought, a cream *tompouce*. Kwibus springs onto my lap and helps me finish it off. On the bridge, the flower seller is packing up for the day. Long shadows follow people as they walk or cycle home, battered by the wind blowing in from the west. I pour myself a cup of coffee and open the envelope that Annie gave me. Kwibus rubs his head against my hand as I read.

The next morning, I dress, as usual, and secure my long grey hair in a bun. I put the folded letter in my coat pocket and walk to Dam Square and into the lobby of the Krasnapolsky Hotel. A stern-looking waiter in a dark suit directs me toward the winter garden. I sit down on a semi-circular sofa covered in green moquette and order an Irish coffee. The wrought-iron structure that supports the glass roof looks like a starving person's rib cage. I shiver. A clatter of breakfast plates brings me back to the present.

A woman walks across the marbled floor. The beige coat she wears is either a size too big, or it fitted once, and she has lost weight. Her tan shoulder bag is expensive and packed to bulging. She smiles and waves, plumping up her curled hair as she walks toward me. We shake hands and introduce ourselves.

"I expect you're wondering why I wrote to you and asked for this meeting." Her accent is Polish.

"Well, I *am* curious."

The waiter brings over my coffee and takes Mrs. Lewandowska's order.

A film of glistening sweat covers her face, and she takes a handkerchief out of her bag and dabs her forehead. "This time of life, you know."

I frown. Women shouldn't talk of such things.

She clicks open her handbag again and shows me a folded article of clothing. The dark stripes are faded, but the sight of them tightens cords around my throat.

"No, I'm sorry, I have to leave now." I stand up and beckon the waiter over.

"Please, stay." She puts her hand on my arm. "There was goodness amongst the horror. You of all people must know that. Look, you sewed this pocket on my tunic." She turns the garment inside out.

"Put it away, please!"

"Why should *we* hide the past away? This is *your* stitching. We all knew it was the Dutch prisoner who sewed the secret pockets. We even had a slang term, calling our pockets Dutchies."

My raggle-taggle stitches are grey now. They conjure the north wind that blew through the sewing workshop and the skeleton rattle of the machines as the coarse linen rasped my fingertips.

Mrs. Lewandowska takes my hand in hers, a sudden intimacy that I'm not ready for. Tears thrum against my throat.

"This pocket helped me survive, Mrs. Jacobs. *You* helped me survive." As she leans toward me, I recognize her perfume from the envelope.

It isn't unpleasant, but even so, I inch away. "My husband, Lenny, was in a concentration camp too. Survivors don't need words, he always used to say. And when he was alive, we promised each other we wouldn't talk of—the—the *old days.*"

"Of course, I respect that, but Annie explained to me that you never sew anymore, and I thought that was sad and wrong." She takes a sip of coffee, and I notice how her wristwatch hangs loosely on her wrist. "Perhaps it was selfish of me to rake it all up again, but I wanted to meet you so much. I needed to see you and thank you. Any act of kindness in that place was a benediction. And now, well, I am very sick, and this is my last chance to meet you." She lets go of my hand, wipes away a tear, and refolds the threadbare uniform.

"Why did you keep it?"

"It may sound odd, but I loved that pocket. In the camp I put little pieces of bread in it. Once, I even smuggled an egg from the kitchen. We keep the things that help us, don't we?"

"Excuse me a moment. I need to powder my nose." In the solitude of the bathroom, sobs zigzag through my body, and I crumple down onto a black and white floor. Mrs. Lewandowska comes in and sits beside me, then hands me a cotton handkerchief and rubs my back as I weep. We huddle together against the frigid air that blasts through ramshackle huts and weaves ropes around us, binding us together back in Ravensbrück.

Her hands are warm when she helps me get up, and her light blouse is now dark with my tears. Like old friends, we walk hand in hand back to the table in the winter garden to collect our coats. We kiss goodbye in the hotel lobby, and I promise to write when Mrs. Lewandowska—Julia—is back in Warsaw.

Above the statue of Atlas on Dam Square, seagulls *scree scree* through the crisp air, their calls a reveille to my soul. I put my hands in my pockets to keep them warm and smile when I recognize a familiar tingle in my fingertips. They are aglow once more, aching for the touch of velvet.

Today is the day. I can't decide what to wear! Finally, after tossing all my clothes on the bed, I opt for simple elegance: a navy-blue pencil skirt and a polka dot blouse with a pussy bow neck that I bought in the Bijenkorf ages ago. I wear my hair loose for the first time in years and put on red lipstick. It is *my* day a little bit too.

Outside, the flower seller is setting up his stall on the bridge. Peony roses are in season—Jocelyn's favorite. I buy a bunch all wrapped up in cellophane with a huge yellow bow to take with me to the Rietveld Academy. In spite of my constant cajoling, Jocelyn refused to tell me what she plans to put in the pocket which I sewed into her jacket lining. She tossed her blonde hair back over her shoulder and said, "Oma, a secret pocket is, after all, a pocket for secrets."

THIS ONE'S NOT FOR US
Farah Ahamed

rolled down my window and watched the street vendors stroll between the stationary cars, tankers, matatus and buses. I had a strange impulse to drive straight into the car in front, just for the satisfaction of knowing I'd made an impact for once. I gripped the steering wheel.

Dilip and I were stuck on Mombasa Road driving to the city center of Nairobi from our offices near the Jomo Kenyatta Airport. We'd just passed the golf course on our left and the old East African railway station on our right. I fiddled with the knobs for the indicator lights and switched off the engine.

A street seller sidled up to the car carrying Kenyan flags of all sizes, the black, red and white fabric flapping around his face.

"Madam, do you need flags, sunglasses or a photo of the president?" he asked.

I shook my head and avoided his gaze to focus on the traffic ahead. He stooped to look into the car. I moved in my seat to block his view.

"What's in the news?" I asked Dilip.

"Independence Day celebrations, Mandela's funeral." He turned the page. "Women activists angry about something or the other."

I glanced at my watch. "I wish the traffic police would do their job. The shops will close soon."

"No point in getting irritated, Resh." He pulled off his shoes, loosened his tie, and covered his face with the paper.

The air was muggy and dense with diesel and petroleum vapors from the industrial neighborhood beyond the railway station and the four wheelers around us. My seatbelt pressed into my middle and cut into my shoulder. I unbuckled it and turned in my seat.

"Be my customer," the seller said. He put on a pair of glasses and positioned the photograph of the president at arm's length. "Life will be better with glasses."

Dilip uncovered his face, yawned, folded the newspaper and laughed. "Here, *kijana*, have a soda." He leaned across and handed him a note.

The man took the money through the window, "*Asante, Mzee.*"

Dilip adjusted his seat to lean back and shut his eyes. "I need a nap."

"Madam, buy *miwani*." The seller held out a pair of dark glasses with a fake Armani logo. "Life will be better. No problem, *hakuna matata.*"

"Oh fine, whatever." I paid him and stuffed the glasses in my handbag.

Sharp police whistles; the vendor swore and, weaving in and out of the cars, disappeared into the bushes. A tout, from the matatu with blaring music parked next to us, leered. I closed my window and turned on the air conditioning.

The lights changed from amber to green. Nothing moved. I took the newspaper from Dilip's lap; he didn't stir. Activists were outraged, I read, at the amendments to the proposed Marriage Bill. I thought of the hire purchase loan Dilip had for the car and the mortgage on our house. If he died or I ever left him I'd be responsible for both.

At the roundabout a few meters ahead, a policeman walked over to a black Toyota and tapped on the window. He said something to the driver, who handed him what I assumed was a license. The policeman pocketed it and walked around the car, his *fimbo* under his arm, kicking each wheel. He stopped by the left front door, opened it, and climbed in.

"Oh my God."

"What's going on?" Dilip sat up and rubbed his eyes.

The driver, a woman in a mustard burqa, jumped out. She stood by her car, hands on hips, her dress billowing around her. The lights changed, cars honked, and those ahead of her started to move. I turned on the ignition, changed lanes, and as we crawled up beside the black Toyota, I rolled down my window. "Do you need help?"

"He wants *kitu kidogo*, some small chai for Christmas. He said he's charging me for wrongful overtaking."

"Let's go," Dilip muttered.

"He's impounded my license," the woman said.

"Oh no," I said.

"Don't get involved," Dilip said. "Drive on."

I moved the car forward and navigated the rest of the way in silence.

At the entrance to the boutique, I turned to Dilip. A shaft of sunlight shone on his clean-shaven head and on the green and blue snake tattoo that ran from his right ear to his shoulder. He patted the jacket pocket where he kept his wallet, phone and glasses.

"I know the dress I want," I said.

"Sure." He buttoned his tight-fitting jacket and, taking a tissue from his pocket, wiped the perspiration off his forehead and the back of his neck.

The boutique, designed like an African hut, had a thatched roof and small windows. On the walls were oddly shaped mirrors and watercolors of flamenco dancers. The clothing was displayed on wrought iron railings suspended from the ceiling by thick chains.

"Is this it?" he said. "It's not what I expected."

"I've seen something here that I like."

He turned to the sales assistant. "My wife needs something appropriate for the Independence Ball."

She looked me up and down. "I'll bring you a selection."

"And the black dress that was in the window last week," I said.

She nodded. Dilip yawned and looked at his watch.

I went into the changing room and fumbled with the buttons on my blouse. The mirror accentuated the lines on my forehead and the traces of grey showing through my short, spiky dark hair. The assistant knocked on the door and handed me several gowns. At the top of the pile was the one I'd set my heart on. It was an off-the-shoulder in black chiffon, with tiny, sparkly, diamanté embellishment. I put it on, and the soft thin material fell smoothly over my hips and caressed my ankles. I stepped out into the shop.

"What do you think?" I asked Dilip, with a self-conscious twirl.

He did a double take and gave a low whistle. "Wow. You look, well, different."

I laughed and swirled again.

He shook his head. "No good."

I stopped. "What? Why?"

"This one's not for us." He folded his arms.

"It is. This is me."

"It's definitely not."

The assistant looked up from folding scarves. "Is there anything else in particular *you'd* like to try on?" she asked me.

"Don't ask her," he said. "I'll decide, that's why I'm here."

I retreated into the fitting room and unzipped the black dress. I pulled on a red satin bubble one with long sleeves, a high neck, a belted waist and an elaborate bow on the left shoulder.

"I need a dress," said a female voice.

I peered through the keyhole and saw a woman in a mustard burqa. I emerged from the changing room.

Dilip nodded. "That's more like it."

"This is annoying me," I said, pulling at the bow.

"You'll get used to it," he said.

"Hello there! Fancy meeting again," the woman in the burqa said.

I turned to face her. "Hello. Did you sort things out with the policeman?" I patted the bow, trying to smooth it down.

"He refused to leave my car," she said, "until I showed him my wallet. Then he took everything from it."

"Oh no! How terrible," I said.

She took off her sunglasses and scrutinized me. "That's a nice dress," she said. "It suits you."

"I think so too," Dilip said, glancing at her. "Doesn't she look perfect?"

"I don't like it," I said.

The woman looked at me. "Well then, get what *you* like."

"I like this one. It's just the dress for you," Dilip said, staring straight at me.

I went back to the changing room and took off the red dress. The assistant tapped on the door. "I'll take whatever you've tried on," she said.

I handed her the black and red dresses and put on a minty green one with a cowl neck and butterfly sleeves.

"Well, what about this one?" I walked toward Dilip.

He stroked his chin. "Nope, never."

"What's wrong with it? Surely it's more flattering than the red one?"

His gaze shifted and I followed it. I wouldn't have recognized her without her burqa. She was as petite and slim as me, but in her early thirties. Her complexion was clear, and her hair, which was curly and long, had auburn highlights.

"That's my black dress," I said. "I've just tried it on."

"Have you? Isn't it beautiful? I love the diamanté."

"That's my dress, that's the dress I want," I said to Dilip. But he was staring at her and did not respond. I waited for a moment and then rushed to the changing room and slammed the door. I sat on the small stool and covered my face. Tears stung my eyes; I brushed them away. This time I wouldn't cry.

I heard voices. I peered through the keyhole: the woman was adjusting the black dress under her arms, looking at her reflection in the mirror. She pouted and twisted to look at her behind. Dilip was watching her. I went down on my knees to see more clearly, but she moved, and only Dilip was in my view.

"That dress looks very nice on you," he said.

She gave a throaty laugh. "Why, thank you. I think so too."

Dilip loosened his tie and ran a finger around the back of his collar. The woman was near him again, still preening. She tossed back her hair and smiled at Dilip. He smiled back.

"Do you think I should get it?" she asked.

A man entered the shop and walked over to her. He was wearing a white baseball cap, faded blue jogging pants and a baggy red T-shirt. Clapped to his ear was a mobile phone. Without interrupting his conversation, he pointed at her, then at his watch and went to the far side of the shop. She looked at Dilip and smoothed the dress over her hips. I got up and changed back into my jeans and blouse.

When I exited the fitting room, Dilip was paying the assistant. The woman was standing by the till, still wearing my dress. "Are you going to buy it?" I said to her.

"I haven't decided." She headed to the changing room.

The assistant handed Dilip the dress wrapped in tissue. "Enjoy the party."

Dilip's mobile rang and he answered it, walking toward the door with the shopping bag. He nodded at me to follow. The changing room opened, and the woman came out in her mustard burqa. She placed the black dress on the counter and pulled her veil over her head as she tucked away her straying curls.

"I've decided," she said to the assistant. "I'll go and speak to my husband." She walked over to the man in the cap, tapped him on the shoulder and held out an empty palm. Without breaking his conversation, he pulled out his wallet and gave it to her. She brought it to the till.

"Excuse me," I said. "If you wouldn't mind, could I please have that dress?"

"I don't understand?" she said. "You already have the one your husband likes."

"I know, but I want this one. I tried it on first, before you."

The woman was quiet for a moment. "No. I'm sorry, I'm taking it."

I looked at the assistant who was concentrating on wrapping the dress. The man in the cap came over. "Did you get what you wanted?" he asked the woman.

"I did." She tilted her head in my direction. "But *she* didn't."

In the parking lot, I noticed a black Toyota parked right behind us. Dilip was leaning against our car, chatting on the phone. I rummaged in my handbag for the keys and noticed the sunglasses from the vendor on Mombasa Road. I put them on and looked around to check for the couple. They were still inside the boutique.

We got in the car and I turned on the ignition. Dilip was laughing at something his caller said. I began to reverse, and the car beeped. In the rear-view mirror, I could see the front bumper of the Toyota. I pressed my foot on the accelerator. There was a resounding crunch and a splintering of headlights.

Dilip dropped his phone and yanked the hand brake. "What the hell are you doing?"

"Serves her right. She was badly parked."

A Statement Bag
Gerri Leen

Someday Amanda Burke will become a clutch girl. She'll abandon the bulky cross-body bags that hold—well, her life, if you come right down to it—and be sleek and stylish and the kind of woman who holds a bag that's made for beauty, not function. A bag in which one carries a phone, a credit card, and maybe a bill or two. And, of course, lipstick—something bright and bold and expensive.

She supposes she'll have to ditch the huge key ring, a brass version of a *Miss Saigon* ticket, and settle for carrying only the keys she really needs. The one to her place, of course, and to her car. But then again, a clutch is for going out. Maybe a car is passé? She's newly divorced and not used to having to worry about designated drivers and which car company to call. She's figured out that cabs are out of fashion but isn't sure whether Uber or Lyft is better.

Cabs always seemed so. . . exotic to her; having someone pull up in a Buick or Honda doesn't seem all that special.

But she's got to join the modern age. At least her phone's up to date, even if she hasn't quite worked up the nerve to add a dating app. She's grateful there are no kids to worry about finding a babysitter for; her friends—none of whom carry clutches, either—tell her horror stories about that.

But there's an app for that now, too. She's seen the ads on TV along with the ones for all those dating sites. How does one sort them out?

She really needs to get on that, because the apartment feels so empty. Mark took the dog with him, saying she's not home enough to be a responsible pet parent. She could hear the implied rebuke: she wouldn't be a good people parent, either.

When they met, he said he didn't want kids. Why is it her fault that he changed his mind and she didn't?

Maybe she should get a cat, but she's allergic to them. Fish might be nice. Do they recognize you? Or a bird. But they're kind of dirty, flinging stuff out of the cage. Or so she's read.

Maybe she should just find a nice guy and settle down again but make double—even triple— sure that he doesn't want kids this time. Make sure he knows that childless is the preferred state. That she is all he'll need, just like Mark was all she needed. That he'll see a beautiful clutch and think, "This is so Amanda," and bring it home just because he enjoys giving her beautiful, impractical things. It might be beaded or have gems or an exotic shell pattern. She'll love it and kiss him fiercely for recognizing her in something so glorious.

Glorious but tiny. They're never big enough to hold sunglasses, and she has really sensitive eyes because of migraine, even on overcast days. She's always got a headache, or she's dizzy. Mark got so tired of her being sick all the time. He used to roll his eyes at all the meds she carries. Sure, she can leave them behind for one night, but can she really be a 24/7 clutch girl?

It would be amazing if she could embrace the effortless elegance while broadcasting the message of "I travel lightly through life." Which is a big fat lie, but she thinks men will find it attractive.

Mark certainly bitched enough about her huge handbags to get the message across. But it had to be big enough to hold her make-up bag, meds, mini-umbrella, hairbrush, and the tin of breath mints. And sunglasses, and the cleaning cloth for her regular glasses. At least one packet of Kleenex, because you just never know. . .

Clutch women probably carry handkerchiefs, which she finds vaguely disgusting. Don't they realize how non-hygienic that is?

Oh, and her bottle of hand sanitizer, too.

Mark always rolled his eyes when she pulled it out. But there are germs everywhere, and —thanks to air travel—they aren't necessarily germs native to the area. And she's sick so much of the time; her resistance is low. Germs laugh when they see her; she has a right to fight back.

Which reminds her of the stun gun. It's small and has a little flashlight on it. Sure, it's not legal everywhere, but she doesn't frequent those places. And while she's never had to use it, and she's read it's only good for use on dogs (the kind that don't let go once they've clamped on), and because you have to hold the thing against a human attacker for quite a long time and people tend to jump away from a shock, still, the thing makes her feel strong and safe.

Well, safer.

She hasn't slept well since Mark moved out with the dog.

Okay, actually, she hasn't really slept at all since he left her, at least, not at home.

Thank God she travels a lot. Hotel rooms feel a lot safer than her home these days. There's only one way into the room, one door to shove a chair under, and one small space to worry about. Not at all like the big, rambling apartment she once had a life in.

A clutch would be stupid for traveling. Her big handbag has travelled all over. She can shove so many things into it, just in case. This is what a clutch can never do: provide security.

But it doesn't need to. A clutch says: "I know who I am, and I know what's coming. I need nothing more than what you see."

She needs way more than that. She's not even sure who she is without Mark and her dog and a life that shouts "we" rather than "I."

She feels she's been left holding all the bad things after the good ones fled. But that can change. She can be more—by carrying less.

She's going to be a clutch girl. Really.

You'll see.

A Weekend with Imogen

Cheney Luttich

It was Friday morning. Sara unlocked the museum door and deactivated the alarm system. She went through the dark lobby and followed the orange glow of the safety lights to the third floor. It was early yet, and all was silent. Only relics spoke—and when Sara closed her eyes and listened—she heard their whispered conversations. She whispered back. She paused and imagined what she must look like if someone were to see her, but she pushed the thought away. Something deep inside craved the comfort and joy that this nurturing provided, so she followed its lead. She felt at home in their quiet world, where there was no noise from the chaotic world outside.

When she reached the third floor, Sara turned on the lights and proceeded to the workroom. She donned a long-sleeved, white cotton lab coat and a pair of white cotton gloves. She walked to the table spread with new acquisitions she needed to catalogue: a few Confederate dollars; a German hymnal; a faded blue calico sunbonnet; and a small, water-stained rectangular cardboard box. She noticed a yellow sticky note with her boss's mix of cursive and print on the box lid and read:

"Sara—Found in storage—needs to be done.
Tag on the box says it belonged to Imogen Haskell—that's all I know.
See you Monday—I'm taking Friday off."

Sara sighed in relief, and her body relaxed. With her chatty boss gone, there was space in the workroom to hear the artifacts' murmurs. Sara hadn't always preferred a quiet workspace, but since arriving at the museum, her desire for silence and to be left alone grew increasingly important to her. Artifacts never asked questions she didn't want to answer, and she never felt pressured to speak of something she wasn't ready to share. Sara smiled to herself. Today, she would pour herself into the world of whispered words and uncover the beauty they were meant to reveal.

Lifting the box's warped lid, Sara murmured to herself. *Okay, let's see what you have for me.* Old tissue paper yellowed with age covered the contents. She lifted the flimsy edges as if they were the middle pages of a book to reveal—folded on top of a skirt—a silver silk moiré taffeta bodice with a pearlescent watered sheen. Delicate tatting trimmed the mandarin collar and flowed in a deep, V-shaped flounce to the bodice's southernmost point. Once a bright, snowy white, the snowflake-patterned lace was now a tea-stained brown, struggling to hang onto the bodice with evaporating threads. A scrolling pattern of grey mercury glass beads covered the rest of the bodice. Some beads were nomadic, having loosened from their knotted roots and rolled their way into the bodice's creases. Sara gasped at the sight of the exquisite piece cradled by the defeated, too small box.

It had been a year since her internship at the state historical society ended. There, in the immense collection of nineteenth century gowns, she immersed herself in the masterpieces of Charles Frederick Worth and Emile Pingat and wrote her thesis on sartorial conspicuous consumption. While life with extant gowns was grand, a historian's reality was not. Job opportunities were few, so the need for a salary and benefits took her to a quaint museum in a rural Midwest world of dusty farms and tiny towns void of nightlife and familiar faces. Its clothing collection was equally small with only a handful of weathered workwear, like the bonnet on the table of items to be catalogued. There were no dolmans with tassels, no embroidered chrysanthemums set in an asymmetrical pattern, no stays made of whale baleen. She knew accepting the position required a sacrifice on her part. There would be no couture clothing and no social life, but she didn't think she'd mind. She thought she could find some professional purpose within the museum's limits and fare well with the occasional trip back to the city to visit friends. As time passed, though, no return trips happened. The thought of the long drive there and back overwhelmed her with incapacitating exhaustion. Instead, she had spent the last twelve months keeping to herself and living a quiet, isolated life. The sight of the bodice, though, with its sprinkling of beads like stars scattered in the night's sky roused what lay dormant and began to revive what had been forgotten.

She carried the box to an eight-foot-long steel worktable, and then put a surgical mask on her face to protect the gown from her breath. Seated, she extracted each rogue bead with tweezers. The clinking sound they made as they dropped one by one—into a metal bowl reminded her of the light chirp of a baby bird. Studying the bodice, Sara dated it as late nineteenth century—either the Second or Third Bustle Period. *Late 1870's or early 1880's, because it's a cuirass bodice.* She studied the line of the fitted right sleeve from wrist to shoulder. Its seam showed signs of thinning from stress. *Possibly worsened by shattering due to the infusion of lead to weight silk.* In the underarm, the moiré's watered effect faded into what looked like a dried slush puddle surrounded by a melting snowbank. *Salt residue from her sweat.*

Sara stood and stretched her aching back. Shedding her gloves and mask, she went to the adjoining reference library room and spent the remaining part of the day searching for information about the petite wearer of this exquisite gown, Imogen Haskell. The one mention of her name was found in a church directory from 1882. There was no record of birth, death, marriage, or children. Imogen clearly existed, but who was she? Sara wondered if she had lived a happy life. Surely, a woman who wore a gown as beautiful as what slept in the cardboard box had experienced something good. Sara found nothing new in the museum's collection of books, microfiche, or computer databases. It seemed no one had felt Imogen was worthy of acknowledgement. If it wasn't for Sara's love of the dress, and her respect for the soul it clothed, Imogen might be lost to the dust of time forever. But that's who Sara was; she felt life when others did not. While it served her well as a historian, it took a toll on her. Each unrecorded life hit her like a boulder to the chest, knocking her down in defeat and bringing on the weight of mourning. There was nothing anyone—not even Sara—could do about it.

When the overhead speaker system announced closing time, she arose and stepped over the stacks of books on the floor that surrounded her chair like a castle wall and walked back to the table before going home for the evening. With the love a mother has for her newborn, she whispered, *Thank you for being here, and for allowing me to get to know you. I'll see you tomorrow.* The gown's lace fluttered from her unbridled breath as if waving in acknowledgement.

The next day, Sara returned to the museum despite it being her day off because she couldn't get the gown off her mind. She wanted to learn more, and it couldn't wait until Monday. Her boss wasn't in, which gave Sara the quiet she needed to explore the gown in the way it deserved. In the silence, Sara heard her heart pound, and she held her breath. She was nervous. It had been a long time since she worked with something so exquisite, and she feared she may have forgotten how to treat such an intimate situation with the care it required. In her white coat, standing over the table, she clasped her gloved hands together as if saying a prayer. *Please tell me if this is hurting you.* Her heart calmed, and with a deep breath, her chest swelled in anticipation. She unclasped her hands and let the muscle memory from her days at the historical society take the lead. Her body knew what to do, and with a gentle, yet firm grasp, took hold of the gown's silk sleeves. With what sounded like a rush of leaves, Sara's arms lifted the bodice from its nest, laid it on the table, and unfolded it to its full length. There, in the middle of the workroom, lay the most beautiful sight—Imogen on display in all her glory. Sara's eyes blinked to keep the tears at bay.

Sara's hands grew in confidence as they led the exploration. The bodice's stays curved in through the waist and then out over what would have been the top of her stomach. The interior boning and seam allowances were bound in grey silk. *Whoever made you took their time.* She traced the curved panels of the bodice lining with her gloved index finger. Inside the sleeves, she found the stains of Imogen's dried and yellow sweat. She looked on the outside of the bodice to view the underarm's discoloration that she had noticed yesterday. *Two sides to the same person.* That is what she loved about her work: an object could present in two different ways if one cared to look closely. Sweat was proof of life, a heartbeat in a shadow of a gown. Did the residue reveal an evening's chase filled with dancing and romance? Did the night's waltz flush her face and color a gray private life? Or did the caked salt reveal a night's panicked chase leaving hidden stains that hardened over time?

Perhaps it was evidence of both. Whichever it was, Imogen was real, and—like the gown's intricate construction—complex.

Sara moved from the bodice to the skirt. She shook her head as she surveyed the damaged silk. There was no doubt that the skirt was suffering from shattering. She imagined how the skirt would have swayed and rustled as Imogen walked into a room wearing it for the first time. What was once a billowing swag of silk, draped around the hips and arranged into a bustle, was now smashed flat. *How long have you been suffocating in that box?* With her fingertips, she attempted to recapture the bustle's previous volume. Weakened from the shredding, the bustle began to collapse under its own weight. She laid it down and patted it ever so gently, as if telling it to rest. It broke her heart, but Sara doubted many late-nineteenth-century gowns would remain one hundred years from now.

Sara proceeded to explore the skirt's insides. She slid her hand, palm facing up, between the front and back hems. She felt the rough of cambric and lifted the skirt's hem to reveal its oval lining and seams. *Wow.* Sara took a step back to grasp the beauty. Despite the deterioration on the outside of the dress, the lined ruffle to protect the dragging hem was intact. Sara rolled the hem upward just enough to where she could see the skirt's deepest parts. Like the bodice, the binding and stitching were perfect. There was enough room below the waistline for Imogen to have worn more than a small bustle pad typical of the natural form period. *First part of the 1880s moving into the third bustle period.* Wire? Mohair? Springs? Sara wondered what type of contraption Imogen preferred to wear to create the protruding fullness that was so fashionable. She unconsciously set her hand on her stomach as she thought of what came with the third, and final, period of the bustle era—the tight boned bodice's pressure and the weight of a wire cage fastened about the waist. She grazed her fingers along the skirt rear's curve and down the seams to where the train tapes hung limp with frayed ends. *No obvious creases. You liked your train to be unrestricted and free.* Envisioning a waterfall of silken bustle created by untied tapes, Sara felt like she could cry. Imogen was both regal and falling apart before her. There was no way to know how much longer before Imogen disappeared into a mound of pieces. Sara felt it was time to call it a day, so she took a large white sheet from the linen closet, laid it over Imogen, and wished her a good night's sleep. That night, she dreamed of Imogen lying on a cold workroom table—exposed and evaporating.

The next morning, she walked from her downtown apartment to what had been the far south side of town more than a century and a half ago. There, she found what had been Imogen's church, long since divided into apartments. She walked around the building and across an alley to a plot of land overgrown with saplings, cottonwoods, and weeds, where she suspected an ignored cemetery lay underneath.

Climbing over both an unruly hedge and a black iron fence, Sara spent the bulk of the day kicking and pulling foliage, revealing one headstone after another. The shift of earth over time had pushed them around. Some leaned backwards about to fall, others tilted sideways as if favoring a limb, while a few sunk into anonymity. After clearing much of the cemetery, she stood back to observe. The unattended headstones marked existence but looked tossed away—discarded—as if the lives they announced were barely worth honoring. Unfortunately, none of the headstones reminded the world that anyone named Haskell had ever lived.

At dusk, Sara let out a sigh, and sat down on a fallen tree branch. She rubbed her throbbing lower back, concluding that there was no more to learn. Imogen's story was over as soon as it began, and—just as Imogen's dress was fluttering away into the breeze of time—so was she. Sara resigned herself to this fact and took comfort in the time they still had together. Imogen was safe at the museum, after all, and would have a proper place to rest. Even though she was deteriorating, Sara was honored to provide her hospice.

Meditating over the past three days, Sara leaned back, setting her hands down on the ground behind her for support. She felt something cool beneath the foliage. Twisting her body so she could look, she saw a small rectangular stone marking a tiny section of earth no bigger than the box that held Imogen's dress. She brushed away the soggy leaves to reveal this engraving:

Elizabeth Haskell
b. January 1885
d. August 1885
Survived by Mother, Imogen

Sara ran her fingers over the engraving while mouthing the words. Pausing, she felt her mind grow foggy and sensed her breath becoming more rapid and her chest heavier. She gasped and rose, never moving her eyes from the words on the stone. Her chest exploded in pain, and her head fell into her hands. "Elizabeth!" she cried. Her body shivered and her chin shook. She curled her body into the small plot of earth before the stone and placed her hands on each side, framing the name. "Oh, God!" She bowed to the name, pressed her forehead against the engraving, and sobbed into the cold stone.

Adrenaline took over while her mind grew even more detached. Her legs began to carry her in a frantic run through the tangles of the cemetery into the downtown sidewalks, now deserted and blanketed in the evening's night. The day's revelation forced the past sixteen months to finally catch up with her. Tears streamed down her face as memories she had buried deep erupted and flashed through her mind in time with her determined footfalls: the discarded plastic pregnancy test in the bathroom trash can— the result of a whirlwind night out in the city with a stranger; the calm on her face in the mirror's reflection when she processed her new reality; the subsequent smile, and the joy that flooded her chest; and the months of excitement she kept for only herself to relish. There was also the list of her favorite nineteenth century children's names with one in particular circled; her leg twitching under the table in anticipation of her and her baby's future while interviewing at the small museum; her squeal of delight in the car ride home after getting the job; and the many long conversations Sara had with her unborn child about what life was going to be like while lying in bed at night, rubbing her stomach. Then there was the moment when five months pregnant—and days before moving to the new town—Sara found herself hunched over the bathroom sink, clenching the edge of the counter because a dagger-like cramping pain pierced her insides. The moment she raised her head and saw her tear-stained face in the mirror, she realized there was nothing she could do. Her white cotton underwear was turning crimson, and her daughter, who she named Elizabeth and called Beth for short, had left her forever.

Sara's body pushed, in desperation, to outrun the memory slideshow. Crying and trembling, she found herself at the museum's door, fumbling with the lock and alarm. Without turning on the lights, she ran to the table in the workroom draped with a white sheet. Her bare hands folded down the top of the sheet to reveal

Imogen's bodice. Her crying slowed as her heart began to throb. Sara needed to be close to Imogen, to this gown, to another mother of a lost child.

Sara positioned her exhausted body on the table under the sheet next to Imogen. She drew Imogen's arm around her left shoulder and rested her right cheek against her beaded breast. She wailed. She placed her left hand on Imogen's lower stomach, then moved it to her own, and then moved it back again to Imogen's. She began to trace her index finger along the beading's scrollwork, which provided a hypnotic respite, and quieted her crying and slowed her gasps for air. She felt a weight lift from her shoulders as she allowed herself to share an unspoken pain. Imogen understood Sara's loss.

Sara slowly got off the table. She folded the sheet with the kind of ceremony reserved for a shroud and set it aside. Carefully picking the dress up next, she placed Imogen's arms around her shoulders. Her tears returned. She tied the sleeves of the dress at the nape of her neck to keep them in place, pulling Imogen close.

She began to dance in slow circles, taking a step between each of her soft sobs. Imogen never let go. The image of her hands framing Elizabeth's name on the stone flashed in Sara's mind as she danced. She wailed again as she tightened Imogen's arms around her neck and buried her face in Imogen's shoulder. Beth was gone, and nobody knew.

The closer Sara was to Imogen, the closer she felt to Beth. She pulled Imogen's arms tighter, drawing Beth nearer. Her feet swirled faster as ebony beads and shredded threads sprinkled the dark workroom's floor like glitter mixed with silk streamers. Sara closed her eyes and drew Imogen closer. The workroom spun. The orange hue of the security lights bled into the black of the room, drenching the dancers in an auburn glow, pricked only by the twinkle from the steel worktable.

There was her daughter. Sara could see Beth now safely on the horizon, sitting upright, smiling, and waving in Sara's direction in the way babies do by repeatedly curling their fingers into and away from their palms. Beth was waiting for her. Sara's feet moved faster still. She tightened Imogen's arms again. Sara's breath grew short and she began to gasp. Her eyes watered as a dizzying ethereal calm blurred everything in the workroom. Beth was within arm's reach, and Sara wanted nothing more than to hold her.

The following Monday, the museum security guard and Sara's boss arrived together. After unlocking the door and disarming the alarm, they headed to the third floor. As the guard made her way through the displays, turning on the lights, her boss went directly to the workroom. The guard had barely finished when she heard a scream. She sprinted to the workroom. Sara's boss ran toward her in terror. "Over there!" she exclaimed, frantically waving her hand in the direction of the desk. The guard turned and discovered Sara; her body entangled in silver silk shreds with two dress sleeves knotted tightly around her neck. Her face was a light shade of icy blue, and her eyes were closed. Her mouth held the faintest shadow of a smile. Sara's arms lay extended with her palms turned outward, ready to receive.

Battle Jacket

Blake Jessop

As bright morning sun shines blindingly into the classroom, Meena squints and shields her eyes with the arm of a loose and formless hoodie. The light breaks for an instant as Mr. Miller crosses in front of the windows. He stops by his desk and fiddles with the CD player. Meena closes her eyes.

"The next romantic poet we'll cover is Samuel Taylor Coleridge. His poems are a lot more narrative than Wordsworth, so I'm sure all of you will be able to stay awake."

Meena lifts her head from the desk, yawns and props her chin in her palms. She actually really likes AP English but starting at 8:30 in the morning is murder. Mr. Miller strolls around the class with handouts. The sheet says *The Rime of the Ancient Mariner - Steve Harris*, followed by a long block of text. Meena rubs her eyes. *Isn't this supposed to be Coleridge?*

"Follow along," Mr. Miller says, returning to his desk and jabbing a finger down on the play button. "We'll read the poem once you get an idea what kind of story it tells."

A sudden cascade of notes pours from the speakers. Cymbals clash and guitars snarl in a low register. Behind the guitars, a bass starts rolling. Meena can't think of a word for what it's doing.

Music isn't a big part of Meena's life. She doesn't mind classical but saying that out loud would get her teased in any high school on earth, whether she's a senior or not. Top 40 radio makes her want to grind her teeth, and her parents—both first generation immigrants from Delhi—only listen to sitar ragas. Meena mostly likes watching movies and reading. The music her dorky English teacher has inexplicably decided to start his lesson with is shattering a dam in her mind that she hadn't known existed. It moves from there to her heart, down into her stomach, and finally to her feet, which start tapping. *Galloping*, she thinks, *the music is galloping.*

The song feels like it lasts twenty minutes, and Meena's heart sails through it. She feels the ship buffet and the beat of the albatross' wings. Hears the click as Death and Life-in-Death dice for the souls of the crew.

What follows is both the most fun and most distracted English class of Meena's life. She finds she loves the poem, which basically has the plot of an 80's horror movie, but that isn't the important bit. The music consumes her in a way nothing has before. The song gallops though her memory in long, lazy circles, and refuses to stop. The bell rings. Meena shoulders her backpack and stops by the teacher's desk.

"Yes?"

"I really liked that song," Meena says.

"I thought Iron Maiden would wake everyone up."

"What I mean is; can I borrow the CD?"

"Sure," her stodgy, old teacher says.

Days pass, then weeks, and Meena waits for the music to fade away like a fad or a crush. It doesn't, and she wonders if she might actually be in love. When she starts seeing Iron Maiden tour posters around town and her heart flutters, she knows. She rarely asks her parents for anything; it feels like they give her enough. Give her everything. She hates asking them to spend money on her and is unsure if it's to keep them happy or because she thinks she doesn't deserve it. The music won't leave her alone, though, so she asks, trying to make it sound like no big deal. It is, as it turns out, a big deal.

"It's final," Meena's father says. Everyone's knives and forks have come to a crashing halt.

"But Dad," Meena begs, "it's a greatest hits tour. They're going to play all my favorite songs. It's not like—"

"Final. You are not going to a rock concert."

Quiet settles on the dinner table. Meena's younger brother is wise enough to keep his head down. Her mother looks disapproving. The only possible source of support is her Uncle Mike.

Mike isn't actually her uncle, but he and her dad have been working together for so long that he feels like part of the family. Everyone older than thirty seems ancient to Meena, but he isn't as old as her father, and mostly acts like an actual human being. He'd been an occasional dinner guest for as long as she can remember, and a source of a lot of illicit movies and ice cream. Meena has no idea why or how he and her father get along.

"Hey, hey," Uncle Mike says, "Deek, no need to argue about it. I'll take her out to the movies next week and we'll forget all about it."

Meena draws a deep, frustrated breath and Mike gives her a look. She doesn't know what it means, so she storms off to her room.

"So, what are we going to see?" Meena asks sullenly. The wiper blades of Mike's old Honda Civic click monotonously.

"Iron Maiden," Mike replies.

Adrenaline floods Meena's brain. "What? Don't joke, seriously?"

"I'm dead serious. The tickets are in the glove compartment."

Meena digs frantically among the maps and batteries and

finds an envelope. Inside are two little strips of life-altering paper that say:

Iron Maiden
Legacy of the Beast Tour
Doors 7pm / Show 8pm

"Holy shit," Meena says, and slaps a hand over her mouth.

Mike laughs.

They park and Mike throws his coat in the back seat. He has an *Iron Maiden* T-shirt on underneath—a threatening zombie dressed as a redcoat and clutching the union jack.

"The Trooper," Meena says. She tugs listlessly at her formless sweatshirt.

"Don't ever let anyone say I don't take care of you," Mike says. He reaches into the back seat and throws a jacket at her. She fumbles it. Fresh blue denim.

"Look on the back."

Meena does. The entire back panel of the jean jacket is obscured by a big cloth patch. A sinister looking pharaoh gazes out at her. He's clad in gold, with a sneering face and Iron Maiden printed in huge letters above his head.

"Classic Powerslave back patch. I ordered it on eBay. The idea is that every time you see a show you buy a new patch and sew it on. I never got around to it and I wish I had."

"Oh my god, thank you!" Meena throws her arms around him and squeezes.

"Okay, now let's go watch some heavy metal. And don't tell your parents."

Winter passes, and surfing the Internet Meena finds that spring is a really good season for metal concerts. She works part time as a lifeguard at the local indoor pool, and her parents get pretty excited when she starts taking more shifts and expresses an interest in saving money. She isn't sure she'd actually go to a concert by herself, but she likes the possibility.

Meena is a senior, and the anxiety of applying to college is acute. The music helps. Every once in a while, she sees someone on TV complain about heavy metal like it's supposed to make her depressed and want to shoot people. That feels as far from the truth as anything can be; the music makes her heart soar, makes her feel like a different, stronger person. Someone less shy, someone cooler and more aggressive. Someone with a dangerous-looking jacket with a cool zombie on it. She researches this new person, and Iron Maiden leads her to a bunch of silly power metal, which is fun but kind of fluffy. It doesn't make her heart skip any beats. She complains about that online, and people keep telling her to go listen to death metal if she's so picky. She does and can hardly believe that she actually likes it.

The day her phone buzzes to notify her that one of the bands she follows is coming to town, she feels the kind of queasy usually reserved for first dates. *Am I doing this? Am I the kind of person who sneaks out to metal concerts?* She stares at the screen. She digs the battle jacket out of her closet. The pharaoh is as tough and immovable as a sphinx.

Meena had worn the battle jacket to school and found it a little hot, so she's pilfered her mother's cloth shears and cut the sleeves off. She doesn't own any band T-shirts, so she just wears jeans, sneakers, a black T-shirt and the battle jacket. She rides the bus, and kind of enjoys people staring at the pharaoh.

Walking into the venue, a bouncer pats Meena down, which she is only just ready for because she watches a bunch of other people go through it like it was no big deal. She wonders how dangerous what she's doing actually is.

Inside are a lot of sweaty white dudes. She's the only brown chick there, so far as she can see, but the battle jacket armors her against isolation. Instead of weird comments or people hitting on her, all she gets is the occasional tap on the shoulder to hear someone say, "Powerslave, sick dude."

The feeling of alienation starts to change when the lights drop, and the crowd starts cheering. Meena feels absurdly young, and not really ready. She stands at the back and watches. The noise is unbelievable, and the lights are bright. The press of bodies changes the sound, making it organic, and she hears little changes, mistakes, improvisations. The vital pulse of the music sucks her slowly forward, as inevitable and dangerous as a riptide. She knows the guys in the band are a few years older than she is—in their 20's—but they look like they could be her classmates.

Meena makes her way to the edge of the mosh pit, a seething mass of people, and pulls the elastic out of her ponytail. She lets the music bob her head as the melody makes waves in her long, black hair.

Over time, the battle jacket gains color. A quilt of names and memories. The little square she got at her first show all by herself has a blue grim reaper, *Children of Bodom*. The next: a group of corpse-painted, grimacing Norwegians above a band name that's totally illegible, but she knows is *Immortal*. Meena has clumsily sewn the patches onto the back of the jacket, but there's no space left without obscuring the pharaoh, which is still her favorite. The front of the jean jacket has pockets and top stitching that make sewing difficult. She has a really cool new patch with a cybernetic spine on it and the words *Fear Factory* in silver thread, but no way to stitch it on without help.

Meena can't figure out whether her parents really don't know what she's doing or if they've just very selectively decided not to notice. Her mother is unbelievably good with a needle. She could help, but Meena isn't sure she wants to come out and be the person she's been right out in the open where her parents can see. She thinks about that first show Uncle Mike took her to. He didn't ask. Didn't feel weird. He just did it.

Meena takes off her headphones, abandons her bedroom, and finds her mother in the kitchen. She dumps the battle jacket on the table.

"I'm really not good at this and I need your help. Can you teach me how to hand-stitch?" she asks. She isn't really sure what her mother will say, or how badly this will go. It feels like confessing to something.

"Let me find my thread," her mother says.

The effect of getting a Doc Marten to the face is a lot worse that Meena expects. She's shorter than most people in mosh pits, so crowd surfers mostly go over her head, but some combination of bad luck, gravity and tremolo picking conspire to join somebody's boot to the side of her face.

Everything goes hazy and Meena falls. The battle jacket doesn't do a lot to cushion the impact. She hits the concrete on her back, and a sea of feet pummels the ground around her. She tries not to imagine what getting trampled to death would feel like.

Instead of being crushed, the feeling of lightness she usually gets when the music picks her up comes back. A hand grabs her arm. Another latches onto the shoulder of her jacket. More grab her elbows, her belt, the front pockets of her jeans.

Meena is hauled to her feet as weightlessly as an angel ascending into the heavens. All around her people make space, even in the crush.

"Are you okay?" a hazy face yells. Meena feels something gritty in her mouth and spits into her palm. Little flecks of white that might be bits of her teeth. She shakes her head, *No, I am not okay.* This, apparently, is when the fun stops, when the heady love affair ends and reality reminds her that this entire idea is stupid, and that the battle jacket is no armor against anything.

The dude who yelled the question gestures to the crowd around them, and they hoist Meena into the air. Normally there's a system for this. You judge if it's a good song for crowd surfing, check the density of people, and ask for a boost. The crowd makes all those decisions for her. Meena is borne up and passed forward, her weight distributed on dozens of hands. On the way she gets a really good view of the band. They're playing *Violent Revolution*, and she remembers she loves that song. In a dizzy, drunken way, she starts enjoying herself.

As the metalheads hand her over the barrier to security, she reaches up toward the band. Someone on stage, hidden by the lights, squeezes her hand as she goes by.

Home in her room, running her tongue over the jagged ruins of three of her teeth, Meena wonders what to do. She seems to have gotten at least a little lucky: none of the broken bits hit a nerve and she's not bleeding. There is absolutely no way to not deal with this, however, and the thought of asking her dad for help makes her stomach churn. There's no way out of the conundrum, so she texts Uncle Mike.

You have to take me to the dentist. :(

In a few seconds her phone buzzes.

What happened?

Meena relates her tale of woe.

Ouch, Mike texts back. *Well, that's kind of the cost of doing business. Everything fun is a little dangerous.*

I cannot tell my Dad about this. He paid for my braces.

Sure you can, Mike replies, *he has good insurance and this sounds expensive.*

I can't. He will be so, so mad. You have to help me.

Her phone stays quiet for a bit.

Okay, so you want me to drive you to the dentist in my 15-year-old Honda and pay all your bills out of pocket?

Meena realizes how dumb that sounds when you just say it. She emits a huge sigh. Her jaw aches and her ears are still ringing. Whether from the music or the head trauma, she isn't sure.

He's going to kill me.

It takes a minute for Mike to text her back. Finally, her phone hums on the pillow beside her head.

You wanted help, here it is: tell your dad. He's not a bad guy. It'll be fine.

Meena's father takes her to the dentist and doesn't say a word for the whole ride over. Meena wears the battle jacket to the appointment. It now has some rusty little stains on the lapels. This has the making of a really big fight, but Mike was right; she's still on her dad's insurance, so they don't have a choice.

A lot happens during the silent ride. Her dad obviously wants to give her a hard time about the clandestine heavy metal habit, but Meena recently announced that she had chosen a college. It's not that close, and he might actually be feeling something about it. Meena wants to apologize for making trouble but can't bring herself to feel like she's done anything wrong. Her grades are great, and the soothing monotony of discordant Djent guitar harmonies has powered her into several scholarships. Meena doesn't throw any of that in his face. Her father doesn't give voice to any of his recriminations. By the end of the drive, the silence feels less like tension and more like a truce.

"How did this happen?" Meena has had the same dentist since she was nine. His name is John.

She taps a patch with a Lovecraftian monster on it that appears to be holding its own head.

"Kreator," she mumbles through the gauze, and gets a confused look. "German thrash metal."

Meena tries not to dwell on the actual dentistry. It hurts. She wonders if music is worth this kind of pain. She tugs anxiously at the corners of the jacket while her mouth gets manipulated. She finds the answer is actually pretty obvious. *This is going to make a good story, just not now.*

When they leave the dentist Meena's mouth is frozen, so she

can't really say much. Her dad opens the minivan door for her. She gives him a long hug, and they go home.

In a new city, feeling at once displaced and excited, Meena searches for her tribe. Fewer bands tour college towns, but she finds a listing for an act she's never heard of called *The Hu*.

That turns out to be Mongolian folk metal. She stands around with her people, dancing and cheering, and none of them can understand a single word because the singer doesn't know any English. She makes friends, buys a beer that she is almost legally allowed to consume, and feels at home. Feels like she's part of something organic that would live on without her but is a little stronger now that she's there. She listens to the resonant thrum of throat singing and revels in the extreme weirdness of horsehead fiddle solos, feeling like a different, more evolved version of herself. Like the battle jacket isn't just armor, or a uniform covered in badges of rank. It feels like the new colors of her soul, new skin, new stripes. The colorful markings of an angrier and more confident version of herself. Not the same girl in the hoodie in AP English class.

This, she realizes, *is a long way from that.*

Meena smiles and heads off to the merch table to see if the Mongolians brought any patches with them from the Steppe.

42ND STREET
SHUTTLE
Linda Welters

Maggie and Tricia exited the auditorium at the Fashion Institute of Technology, relieved that the conference was finally over. It had been three days of papers and panels in a dark auditorium with slides on a screen. The technology of fashion was the theme, and speakers from both industry and academia had presented their work. Tricia had given a paper on new elastic fabrics for 1930's swimsuits. Now that the conference was finished, they could relax and be tourists for a day in the Big Apple before heading back to their respective hometowns.

On this warm day in May, Maggie wore a Liz Claiborne dress, which made her feel very fashionable in the big city. Liz Claiborne, Anne Klein, Evan Picone—these were aspirational labels for professional women in the mid 1980's. On her assistant professor's salary, the dress had been a bit of a splurge. It was an olive-green shirtdress with dolman sleeves and large shoulder pads that made the prominent shoulders balance the long, wide mid-calf length skirt. A big red patent leather belt cinched Maggie's waist. She accessorized the look with a necklace of painted ceramic beads that she had made herself. Tricia, on the other hand, wore an oversized white linen blouse over linen pants the color of oatmeal. Her wardrobe preference was top quality fabrics in neutral colors.

The weather was cooperating, with no rain or wind in the canyons of New York City. It felt great to be outdoors. The two colleagues, who had met at a previous conference, walked to Manhattan's east side to catch the subway uptown. As fashion historians and art lovers, a visit to the Costume Institute at the Metropolitan Museum of Art was a must. "Man and the Horse" was the theme of the current exhibition, and both women wanted to view the tailored jackets, riding habits, and resplendent uniforms that likely made up the breadth of the show.

Later that afternoon, after leaving the museum, Tricia suggested a foreign film for the evening activity. The small college town in Ohio where she lived only showed major Hollywood studio releases. Maggie, who could easily get to Providence for art films, pushed for the theatre. She knew that Sam Shepard's new play, "Fool for Love," had opened off-Broadway at the Circle Repertory Company. Maybe they could score some last-minute tickets. Since Maggie had set her heart on the play, Tricia decided to go along. They walked three blocks from the Met's Fifth Avenue entrance to Lexington Avenue, where they entered the subway, transferred at Grand Central, and caught the shuttle to 42nd street so they could buy discounted tickets from the TKTS booth in Times Square.

The shuttle was not as crowded as a typical Saturday afternoon, but Maggie and Tricia could not find seats. They stood in the middle of the car holding onto a vertical pole for the 90-second ride. As the train started moving, the air conditioning kicked on. The moving air slowly filled out Maggie's skirt, lifting it out just like Marilyn Monroe's in *The Seven Year Itch*. Maggie tried holding the front of the skirt down with her right hand, but that made the back lift even higher. She thought of her underwear, wondering if it soon would be revealed to all. Try as she might, the skirt would not stay down.

A middle-aged man sitting at the end of the car was taking great delight in the ballooning skirt, watching it flare out. He laughed and smiled at Maggie. Maggie studied him, observing him: skin the color of coffee milk; the gray at his temples; the work shirt and jeans; the scruffy sneakers. She held his gaze and smiled back. What else could she do? He didn't look harmful and the ride was short. The skirt situation might get worse if she moved down the car. She resigned herself to having to wait out this Marilyn moment until the train rolled into 42nd street.

Tricia, meanwhile, was mortified, and kept looking away. Why was this guy laughing and smiling so much? Maggie saw that Tricia was nervous about this embarrassing incident going on too long. Maybe she was wondering if the man would follow them out of the train. Seconds passed, then a minute. It seemed interminable, this billowing skirt. Finally, the train slowed, and the skirt deflated. The man looked dejected. His expression was like that of a child when the magic show ended. The doors opened and the passengers started filing out. As Maggie and Tricia moved to exit, the man looked at Maggie and said, "You would have loved me once." Maggie looked back, surprised. "When I was a soldier," he said. Maggie felt sad for him. Was he a Vietnam vet? Where was his home? How was it that he could fall for a stranger on a train? She ruminated on what he'd said: "When I was a soldier." They'd just come from an exhibition replete with military-inspired riding outfits and paintings of warriors in splendid uniforms. What happens, she thought, to the tender-hearted ones not meant for fighting?

Maggie and Tricia ascended the dank stairway, catching the whiff of urine as they emerged onto the street and headed to the TKTS booth. Neither woman said anything about the incident. Maggie patted down her dress, no longer so enamored of its big wide skirt and bright red patent-leather belt.

THE
WEIGHT
OF
A
BAG
Gabriella
Brand

"**Y**ou gotta get a bag," Sandy had said. "You can't start junior high in September without a bag."

It was August of 1958. The two girls were walking home, each holding a cherry Popsicle that dripped onto the sidewalk. They had been to the town swimming pool together and were just rounding the corner of Sandy's street.

John Davenport Junior High wouldn't start for another week or so, but Sandy insisted that Anna-Maria's lack of a handbag was a pressing issue. Sandy had already bought one.

Back in elementary school, there was no need for a handbag. No one carried anything. They didn't need money for lunch because everyone went home at noontime, on foot or by bicycle. And, of course, no one wore lipstick. But now things were different, Sandy explained.

"If you don't have a bag, where are you going to put your *Clear-Skin*? Huh?"

At the beginning of that summer, Sandy suggested that Anna-Maria squeeze the occasional blackheads that had begun to appear on her nose, and that she slather her skin with acne cream.

Sandy always knew what to do, what to buy. She kept her eyes on the older girls in town, and especially their accessories: charm bracelets; pennies in loafers; oversized safety pins on plaid skirts.

"For a bag, you need something cool," explained Sandy. "Like a feed bucket or something."

Anna-Maria had no idea what a feed bucket was, but she

concluded it was a type of purse. Sandy's knowledge of the world was vaster than anyone Anna-Maria had ever met. Sandy knew, for instance, that Rock Hudson was double-jointed, and that Elvis Presley would eat five scoops of ice cream before he did "it" with a woman. Sandy claimed to have read these facts in movie magazines, the ones with black and white photos that were sold in the darkest corner of *United Cigar and Newstand*, right next to the humidors.

Anna-Maria wondered where Sandy had learned about feed buckets, but she didn't want to ask. She worried Sandy would claim that feed bucket bags were common knowledge, like the fact that Marilyn Monroe slept naked.

"Do you think I can get one at Clemen's?" asked Anna-Maria, mentioning the local clothing store on Main Street a few blocks away. Clemen's featured women's sweaters that got dustier as they stood in the sun-baked front window all year long.

"Not a chance," shrieked Sandy. "Go out to the Rossinger's and buy a decent bag."

Anna-Maria sighed. It wasn't that easy to get to Rossinger's. The department store was fifteen miles away in a shopping center off a major highway. But Anna-Maria's mother didn't drive and asking Father would be tricky.

"Rossinger's, huh?" asked Anna-Maria, wondering how she would ever get out there.

"Show me your bag the minute you buy it," said Sandy, turning and waving goodbye as she headed up her driveway.

"I will," said Anna-Maria, crossing the street to her own house.

The closer it got to the first day of school, the glummer Anna-Maria felt. She went out of her way to avoid her neighbor but was grateful for Sandy's advice to make sure her lunch money was tucked into her sock. And Sandy had already led Anna-Maria to the drugstore next to *United Cigar* where they had browsed the aisles for lipstick. Sandy chose a tube of *PinkNOrange* for Anna-Maria, and *French Spice* for herself.

"You gotta blot it against a tissue, like this," Sandy demonstrated by kissing a folded paper napkin.

Anna-Maria had hidden the *PinkNOrange* in the far back corner of her top bureau drawer so her mother wouldn't find it. She knew she'd have to prepare her mother for the eventual sight of pink lips as garish as a snow monkey's. Anna-Maria's mother liked serious things. Classic things. European things. Unlike the other women in the neighborhood, she never wore pants and kept her long hair wound in a tight chignon, as if she had to read a dissertation in front of the French Academy every day. When walking into town to the hairdresser or grocer, her pace was always solemn and slow.

Anna-Maria began to plot a strategy to convince her mother about going to Rossinger's for the all-important handbag. It wasn't a matter of money. It was more a question of silliness. Would her mother place this request in the category she called "nonsense," where she stored other things like baby doll pajamas, Popsicles, *American Bandstand*, poodle skirts, and Twinkies? And breakfast cereals other than oatmeal, too. It was no good whatsoever to argue that other kids ate spongy cylinders filled with sugar. Anna-Maria's mother didn't care.

"That's not food. It's nonsense," she said.

At times, she would launch into a long speech about "the old country," a place where Anna-Maria had never been and didn't want to go. In her imagination it was always grim and fractured by war, with not enough meat and butter to go around.

Once, her mother had caught Anna-Maria with a slick movie magazine that Sandy had lent her.

"Why are you reading such a thing?" she asked. "It's nonsense." Anna-Maria was sure that her school handbag would fall into this large category.

But that night at dinner Anna-Maria got up her courage as she sat at the table with Father and Mother on either end. She knew better than to start off with, "Sandy says," and decided to present her need for a handbag as a matter of practicality.

"There's going to be a lot to carry around in seventh grade," she began.

"Why is that?" asked Father, as he passed a plate of green beans sautéed with mushrooms.

"Um. . . because I'll be staying at school for lunch. So, I have to bring lunch money."

"Don't you have a change purse?"

"Um, yeah, but I'm afraid it might get lost. Because it's small. And besides, I need lots of pencils and erasers," said Anna-Maria.

Her parents looked puzzled.

"Because I'll move around from class to class. I won't have a fixed desk," she explained. "And I'll want to be. . . really. . . prepared."

Mother nodded, smiling at the thought of such a studious and prepared daughter.

Anna-Maria felt as if she may be on the right track.

"So, just get a zippered pencil case," said Father.

"Yes, yes, okay," said Anna-Maria, picturing it lying at the bottom of her feed bucket bag.

"But I also need to bring. . . well. . . some other stuff," she added, glancing at her mother and hoping for a sign of feminine understanding that would prevent the need to utter "sanitary pads."

Mother said nothing while sweeping crumbs off the table into her hand with a little brush.

"Actually, I was thinking of a bag. Like a handbag," said Anna Maria.

"Oh, that's a good idea," said Mother, bringing melon to the table for dessert. It was beautifully presented, scooped into perfect rounds and topped with a bit of mint.

"I suppose it is," said Father.

As they finished the melon and the conversation drifted, Anna-Maria thought it best to save the discussion of Rossinger's for another time.

After the dishes were washed, Mother asked Anna-Maria to follow her upstairs.

"I have some handbags you can choose from," she said.

Anna-Maria gulped. Her mother opened her closet doors, revealing the Swiss precision of the organized contents. There were navy blue skirts in one section, gray in another, and all the shoes were carefully paired in little boxes. Mother began to take leather handbags off of a high shelf.

"Here, this one is nice. It has a good handle."

Anna-Maria stared at her Mother's old handbag, a black patent leather with a brass clasp. She remembered her mother carrying it to Anna-Maria's ballet recital a few years ago.

"Um. . ." she said, gulping.

"Or what about this one?" asked Mother, handing her daughter a navy-blue one with a zippered top.

"A zipper would be useful for keeping everything inside," said Mother.

Anna-Maria knew her mother was trying to be helpful.

"I was kind of thinking of something like. . . um. . . a feed bucket," she said.

"What's a feebucka?" asked Mother, her European tongue

tripping over the unfamiliar word.

"Um. . . it's a kind of bag," said Anna-Maria, "that holds a lot."

"Well, this one holds a lot, too" said Mother, handing Anna-Maria yet another bag, a brown leather affair with two long handle straps and a little silver chain that dangled off of the end of one handle. It was the color of sludge.

Anna-Maria gingerly brought up the possibility of Father driving her out to Rossinger's.

"I don't think that's necessary. We already have several bags right here. You just need to choose one," said Mother.

Anna-Maria knew when she was defeated. "Waste not, want not," said Mother, who seemed to be warming up for one of her little speeches.

Not wanting to hear about some European relative who had been so hungry during the war that he ate the soles of his own shoes, Anna-Maria thanked her mother and ended up accepting the brown leather bag with the long straps. She went up to her room, threw herself on her bed, and buried her wet face in the pillow.

Meanwhile, Sandy pestered Anna-Maria every afternoon of the week leading up to the start of school.

"Have you gotten your bag yet?" her friend asked as the two girls walked to the town pool before it closed on Labor Day.

"No," Anna-Maria lied.

"You'd better hurry," counseled Sandy. "All the good ones will be gone."

The night before the big day, Mother softened the brown leather with saddle soap and cleaned the silver chain. Anna-Maria reluctantly filled her hand-me-down bag with pencils, lunch money, a new pink eraser, two small packages of Kleenex, a big tube of hand cream, and the previously hidden lipstick. The brown bag seemed like a weight on her arm, on her spirit.

"You look so mature," said Father, as Anna-Maria left the house for the first day of school.

She walked slowly toward Sandy's house. The bag felt awkward on her arm. She couldn't decide whether to throw the long handles over her shoulder or not, and it already felt too heavy. Maybe she shouldn't have put the big tube of hand cream in.

Sandy came bounding out of her house and raced towards Anna-Maria.

"Oh, you finally got a bag. Let me see!" she shouted.

Sandy looked the bag over inside and out, scrunching up her face as if she were handling a dead dog. She ran her hands over the smooth exterior, still a bit sticky from the saddle soap, and pulled on the silver chain.

"Did you get this at Rossinger's?" she asked.

"Yes, um. . . no, in the end I got it somewhere else."

"Where?" asked Sandy, scowling. "It's really weird. You should have let me come with you."

"Well, my. . ." Anna Maria started to answer.

Fortunately, before Anna-Maria could to finish her sentence, she and Sandy were joined by a gaggle of neighborhood girls. Anna-Maria eyed the other girls' purses. There were a lot of feed buckets. Maybe Sandy had talked to them, or maybe feed buckets were really common knowledge.

Anna-Maria waited for Sandy or one of the other girls to make fun of her bag, but Sandy got caught up explaining to everyone how to put pennies in their loafers. Apparently, they were all doing it wrong.

"I saw a bunch of eighth graders at the shoe department at Rossinger's, so I know," said Sandy.

"It's not cool to put a penny in each side," she continued. "You need to put one penny in the right-hand slot if you already have a boyfriend, and in the left if you're still looking."

If a girl had put in two pennies, Sandy urged her to take one out.

As soon as the loafers were in order, the group headed down the street, crossed the intersection and approached John Davenport Junior High. Anna-Maria's palms were moist, and the brown bag kept slipping from her grip.

She and Sandy weren't in any of the same classes, and after going over their schedules they agreed to find each other in the cafeteria at lunchtime.

As she made her way from class to class, Anna-Maria felt a mixture of anxiety and pride. The constantly changing classes, crowded hallways, and independence needed to get from one place to another were all so different from elementary school. And yet she made it to each class on time, and always had a pencil ready.

In third period history class, a girl she didn't know asked if she had any tissues, and Anna-Maria was happy to rummage through her well-stocked brown bag and hand the girl one of the two packets she had brought. She and the girl talked a bit before the teacher arrived. The girl didn't make any comment about the weirdness of Anna-Maria's purse.

Throughout the morning, Anna-Maria found that she wasn't thinking about her old friend Sandy at all. By noon, it actually felt good to be walking around on her own, without Sandy's constant jabber and advice. And somehow, carrying the big bag made her feel older, and even a little wiser.

At lunchtime Anna-Maria could see Sandy sitting at the head of a cafeteria table, surrounded by some of the neighborhood girls. Anna-Maria placed her cafeteria tray down and listened to Sandy's monologue about someone in one of her classes who was wearing really childish shoes.

"Like tie-ups. They look like something you'd wear in third grade," pronounced Sandy.

The other girls laughed.

Anna-Maria ate her lunch quietly. She didn't know what was so wrong with tie-up shoes. After all, she'd been wearing tie-ups herself up until last year.

When the bell rang, Sandy and the other girls walked out together, like a herd of heifers heading out to pasture. They pushed open the big double doors and proceeded into the corridor.

Anna-Maria walked a bit with them, then hung back to stop at the water fountain.

A few ninth-grade girls, coming from gym class, got into line behind her.

"That's the coolest bag," said one of the older girls, leaning over Anna-Maria's shoulder and gesturing toward the brown bag. The girl was tall and blond, with suntanned cheeks and no lipstick.

"Hey, Terry, look at this cool bag," said the girl, turning to her friend and pointing to Anna-Maria's purse.

"Yeah," said the girl named Terry. "It's definitely neat."

Anna-Maria was stunned. At first, she stared down at the floor, overcome with shyness. Then she looked up and realized the older girls were smiling at her.

"Thanks," she said in response to their compliments. She stopped short of telling them the bag's origin.

As she stepped aside to let the next girl move to the water fountain, the girl named Terry kept chatting with Anna-Maria.

"You're in seventh, right?" said the girl. "I remember my first day. Don't worry, it all gets better," she said with a smile.

"Yeah," said Anna-Maria, "I hope so."

As she walked away, Anna-Maria noticed that Sandy had joined the water fountain line and had seen her interaction with the ninth graders. She waited for Sandy to grab her arm and give her a piece of advice. But Sandy just stared at Anna-Maria, her eyes narrowed and her mouth open in surprise.

Suddenly Anna-Maria felt light and weightless.

She nodded at Sandy, then swung the brown bag easily onto her shoulder and went off to her next class.

HEMLINES

P.J. Schaefer

*L*et it go, Tricia told herself as—while staring at her daughter, Alannah—a memory arose of her late father's voice, which still rattled her nerves as if he stood before her that very second. "Right now!" he had commanded. "It's indecent. You're transmitting a message!" Tricia had hurriedly unrolled the band of her pleated, plaid skirt until the hem dropped to cover her knees. She had cursed herself then for entering the house before reversing the daily high school ritual of making the garment into the miniskirt it was not. Tricia shifted her attention back to Alannah, who openly strutted about the kitchen in a navy, spandex miniskirt that barely covered her derriere.

"Alannah," Tricia began, attempting to sound only casually interested, "is that a new outfit?"

Alannah reached for a cereal bowl as she replied. "No, not really. I've just adapted it to make it more stylish. Why?"

Tricia checked herself before she spoke. The balance between criticism and getting her sixteen-year-old daughter to correct something often turned on a single word or a subtle tone of voice. "Oh, I just haven't seen it before." Tricia paused. "It's a bit nippy out there this morning. Your legs might get chilly quickly."

Alannah looked out the window. "Hmm. I'll just wear my long coat then, and maybe my black boots."

Tricia had to stop herself from saying, "Like the go-go girls of the sixties?" Instead, she remained quiet until Alannah finished her breakfast and moved to the doorway to leave for school after donning her coat. "Have a good day, and be careful out there," Tricia said as she kissed her daughter on the cheek.

Be careful out there, Tricia mentally repeated to herself, fearful about the steps her daughter had already taken toward danger. She watched as Alannah closed the door firmly behind her.

Only minutes later, Tricia closed the same door and drove to the office where she worked. A human resources director for a small medical supply company that provided oxygen to facilities and individuals, Tricia always arrived before anybody else. She enjoyed those quiet moments before the day officially began as well as the chance to observe the way her employees filled the office and started their day. That day, she had not expected to find Amanda Cartright sitting outside her office, barely in control of her tears.

"Amanda? What's wrong? What can I help you with this morning?"

Amanda kept her face turned to the carpet and mumbled, "Not in the hallway. Can we talk inside, please?"

Tricia nodded, unlocked her office door, and stepped aside as she gestured for Amanda to enter. "Coffee?" she asked.

Amanda shook her head, turned to close the door, and cleared her throat. "Do we have a dress code or policy here of which I am not aware?"

Tricia stopped mid-stride on the way to her desk. "No, not really. The employee handbook states only to 'dress professionally except on designated dress-down Fridays in July and August.' Why do you ask?" Tricia queried as she deposited her briefcase on the desk and took her seat behind it.

Amanda stood, walked the length of the office and back again, twirled in a circle, and asked, "Would you say I am dressed 'professionally'?"

Tricia examined Amanda's four-piece ensemble—jade skirt,

blazer, vest, and cream-colored shell—worn that day with two-inch spiked heels. The clothing fit as if tailor-made for Amanda. The skirt rose about four-and-a-half inches above Amanda's knees, its hem just slightly above mid-thigh. *Can I not escape the mini-skirt today?* Tricia wondered briefly as she took a closer look. She decided not to commit to an answer until Amanda offered additional information. "Please sit, Amanda. Again, why do you ask?"

Amanda sank into the chair and dabbed at her eyes with the tissue she held in her right hand. "Well, my supervisor, Anne Redding, told me it's my own fault because of the way I dress."

Tricia felt her stomach clench. "*What* is your own fault? What is *it*?"

Amanda cleared her throat again. "Well, I'm not trying to get anyone in trouble or anything. I didn't start by coming to you. I wanted my supervisor to help, but she just said it's my own fault."

Tricia nodded. "Your fault that . . ."

"That Brad Simmons keeps making me uncomfortable."

"How does he do that, Amanda?"

Amanda remained silent for several minutes, shifted in her seat, and finally spoke. "He makes crude remarks and dirty jokes. He brushes against me as if we're in a tight hallway."

Tricia opened a drawer in her desk, took out a pad and pen, and started writing even as she asked, "He's done this how many times? Once, several, many?"

"Many."

"And you have asked him to stop?"

"Yes, of course I did. I told him he's making me uncomfortable about coming to work." Amanda stared at her lap as she pulled the tissue into small pieces. "I've actually skipped work a couple of times because I didn't want to face him. That's the reason I finally went to Anne Redding. I didn't want to lose my job because of my absences."

"I see." Tricia knew what other questions she had to ask, regardless of her innate reluctance. "And have you ever had any kind of relationship with Brad outside of work?"

"No."

"Has he ever demanded that you go out with him or become intimate with him?"

"No, no, but he's always making suggestive remarks about me and my anatomy."

Tricia scribbled additional notes on her pad. Experience had taught her to record nothing on the official computerized forms until granted permission.

"What action do you seek here, Amanda? Do you want to file an official complaint, have Brad fired, get transferred, sue Brad, sue the company? What, exactly?"

"I don't really want any of those things. I just want Brad to stop creeping me out so I can come to work without worrying about him bothering me." Amanda's gaze rose from the floor back up at Tricia. "And, I want my supervisor to stop criticizing my attire and telling me that 'wearing a miniskirt is just asking for trouble.'"

Tricia nearly flinched at the echo of the very words she had considered using that morning. "Well, I'll be talking to Anne and Brad as soon as I can today, but how about I move you over to Accounts Payable for the day? Chelsy Lakeland will not be in, so you can cover her spot. That way, you will not be near either of them."

Amanda nodded her consent and waited while Tricia made calls to set-up the substitution, and then left.

Tricia searched her memory for Brad Simmons' work history as she searched for his company file. She also scanned her list of current company openings and job descriptions. She decided to speak with Anne Redding first, since she supervised both Brad and Amanda.

Anne entered Tricia's office ready to defend herself. "So, that little beguiler complained about me? How dare she? She just doesn't get that she brings it on herself, the way she dresses. She has no sense of women's history, how hard we fought to be viewed as more than our bodies, while all she can do is show hers off. This is a place of business, not a brothel."

Tricia waited before replying. Anne Redding had worked at the company since high school, having started in the mail room long before Tricia joined the company. She'd held a part-time position during college, even working during semester breaks. Her work ethic and dedication were a given, but harsh judgments of others, at times, were also evident. "Let's keep our language professional; shall we? Does she do her job, Anne? Her performance reviews are fine, but perhaps they lack something I should know."

"Actually, she's smart and efficient, and good at the job. She takes initiative and has even streamlined some of our procedures."

"And how does she work with the male members of your department? Have there been other complaints?"

Anne sighed. "No other complaints from her or from the men. But she frequently comes to work in very short skirts."

"Do they impede her work in any way?"

Anne sighed again. "No, but they might be distracting the men."

Tricia chose her next words carefully. "If men get distracted from their jobs, whose responsibility is that: the men's, or the perceived cause of the distraction?"

Anne remained silent for quite a while. "I take your point." She fidgeted a little in her chair. "So, am *I* fired for bringing up Amanda's clothing?"

"No, but I warn you to avoid such comments in the future. Now, let's talk about Brad. Does *he* do his job well? Have any others complained about him to you?"

Again, silence filled the room. "Well, let's just say he is not without his charms, and that sometimes those charms help him get others to do his work."

"Others, except perhaps Amanda?"

Anne fidgeted again. "Maybe."

"Have you witnessed any of the conversations or behaviors Amanda alleges?"

"Not really, but I do know Brad. He's kind of flirty and cavalier, a proverbial 'man's man,' and he's not used to censoring himself."

After thanking Anne, Tricia summoned Brad to her office. He began the meeting with a broad smile and a double-handed handshake held just a moment too long. Tricia then gave him a questionnaire to complete and scrutinized the answers as he sat silently in front of her.

"Brad," she said, "are you aware of the opening for an inventory supervisor in our supply division?"

Brad hesitated briefly. "Ah, I was not aware. Why are you asking me?"

"Well, I'm thinking of transferring you to that position. It offers the same hours and a slight raise in pay, but at the Smith Street location. Your supervisor and I think you'd be a good fit there."

Brad rose to his feet. "Why? What's going on? Is this about that Amanda chick? Did she complain? She's just ultra-sensitive, that's all. And if she can't handle a little . . ."

Tricia cut him off, though his response reaffirmed her decision about the transfer. "Brad, I'm not firing you. I'm transferring you, and offering you a raise, unless you prefer to be fired." She paused. "And, based on your survey answers, I'm also mandating that you retake the online course on proper workplace comportment."

"But . . ."

"No buts, Brad. It's what's best for you, and for the company. You will like it at Smith Street; it's more of a man's world over there. The supervisor you are replacing will train you for the next two weeks."

That evening, Alannah was just coming through the door after her *a capella* practice when Tricia returned home. Tricia couldn't help but stare again at Alannah's miniskirt.

"What?" Alanna asked. "What now?"

"Why do you do it?" Tricia couldn't help but ask.

"Do what?"

"Wear such tight, short, revealing clothing?"

"Because it looks good. Because it's the style. Because I like it. Because I *can*. All of the above. . ."

"But don't you ever feel like you're just showing off, accentuating your body, as if that's what's most important about you? Do you think it's anti-feminist, anti-women?"

Alannah sat down and stared intently at her mother. "Didn't you try to turn your skirts into miniskirts when you were in high school?"

"Yes, I did. But it was a kind of rebellion. We *were* trying to look sexy too, but, in retrospect, our parents were right; there was kind of a trashy and daring element to it all. We were actually falling into the male fantasy trap without realizing it. Your generation is supposed to be so much smarter than we were."

Alannah sighed. "We *are* smarter. We are *not* you. Our feminism is not *your* feminism. For us, the freedom to dress as we please, to show our bodies, to *celebrate* our bodies if we want to, is actually our strength. We say, 'We can be both bodies *and* brains; respect both.' You believed you were more than your bodies to the point that you denied those bodies." Alannah laughed aloud. "To us, the mini-skirt is just a fashion choice, emphasis on *choice*. We are more than our clothes, but our clothes help us to say so." Alannah stood and moved to give her mother a hug. "Mom," she said, "hemlines may rise or fall, but the women wearing them are on the rise every day; don't you think?"

Tricia chuckled softly. "Maybe," she said as she squeezed Alannah tightly. Deep in her heart, she thought her daughter was already several rungs higher on the ladder of life.

SECOND HAND ROSE

Lindsay
Bamfield

There's a picture of her sister in the family album, aged nine and wearing the spotted dress. The year is 1959, and—although the photo is black and white—she remembers the color exactly: an insipid blue with large white spots. Handmade smocking decorates the bodice in darker blue and white. Mrs. Oliver had made it for Ally's eighth birthday. Ally stands on the lawn, self-consciously grinning into the camera. The dress is already too short on her, so it's destined to be passed on to Lucy, two years her junior.

Lu hates the dress. She couldn't have said whether it is because of the dress itself or because it would be yet another hand-me-down. Most of her clothes have been worn by Ally first, except for shoes, because her mother is fussy about shoes fitting perfectly. Their neighbor once called her Second Hand Rose, "like the famous song." Lu has never heard the song, but she hates it anyway. Mr. Peters always calls her Rose now, so she hates him too.

Lu's favorite dress is made of flimsy, bright pink cotton edged with pale pink rickrack. It is a cheap thing, but Lu loves it because it was new, and she had chosen it. No one had worn it before, which made it all the more precious. It is too tight for her now. When she wore it last, two buttons had flown off as her mother was fastening them down the back.

She recalls her mother's sigh of exasperation when she next puts it on as she tries to make her body smaller. It doesn't work. She seems even larger now.

"Growing girls!" The tone of her mother's refrain suggests this is a bad thing. "Ally needs a new dress, but at least her blue spotty frock will soon fit you."

Grandma is keeping an eye on Lu while her mother takes Ally to buy the new dress. Lu desperately wishes she could have one too, but she knows the hated dress is now hers. She remembers that the dress is hanging in the cupboard on the landing. The cupboard smells of long-ago mothballs.

Lu waits until Grandma's eyes close for her afternoon nap, then creeps upstairs to the cupboard. She opens the door carefully and pulls the dress from its hanger. She bundles it up and climbs the narrow stairs to the attic, taking care to avoid the creaky middle of the third stair. In the attic she lifts the loose floorboard and stuffs the dress down between two joists. It's a safe hiding place. Ally rarely comes up here because of spiders, and her mother says the dust makes her sneeze. Lu doesn't mind spiders and the dust doesn't bother her. She likes the saggy old chair that's stored there, and often brings up her books so she can curl up on the old chair cushions to read.

She is back downstairs making swirly patterns with her colored pens before her mother's key in the lock awakes Grandma. Ally's new dress has a green checked pattern. Lu hates check even more than spots.

"That's odd, I can't find the blue spotty dress," announces her mother a few days later. "It must be about right for you now and you'll need it for the garden fete next month. I can always take the hem up if it's still too long."

"I'll help you look for it," says Lu, making a performance of looking in the wardrobe and the chest of drawers she shares with

Ally. "It must be here." But inevitably, no dress is found.

"She doesn't like my spotty frock," chimes in Ally. Lu worries that Ally has guessed that she has hidden the dress.

"Oh, yes I do," she claims. "Especially the smocking." That bit was true at least. Lu loved the feel of the gathered smocking beneath her hand. "I was looking forward to wearing it at the fete." She squeezes her fingers into a cross behind her back, so the lie doesn't count.

"Your pink one is far too tight," says her mother. "I suppose it'll mean a new one," she adds with a sigh.

Lu hopes her new dress might be red, and she looks forward to the shopping trip, but none is forthcoming. The day of the fete draws near when her mother calls for her to come and try on her new dress. Lu is disappointed that she hasn't gone to town with its exciting shops and—if she were lucky—tea at Forte's teahouse but is thrilled by the news of her own dress. She runs to her mother and sees her holding the blue spotty dress.

"Where did you find it?" Lu knows she will be in terrible trouble. No one else could possibly have hidden the dress in the attic. She decides she will give Ally a pinch later for telling her guilty secret. She looks at her mother's face, but there is neither a frown nor a pursed mouth to signal her disapproval. Instead, she is smiling. Lu fidgets, wondering why her mother hasn't reprimanded her. Her hands feel damp.

"I had Mrs. Oliver make you a new one," says her mother. "Luckily she still had plenty of the material, so now you have your very own blue spotty dress."

Lu takes it and puts it on. It fits perfectly. She runs her hand down the front for the ribbed smocking. Her hand brushes smooth material. She looks down. There is none; her dress is simply an old dull blue with white spots. Her mother notices the gesture.

"Mrs. Oliver hadn't got time to do a smocked top before the fete. Besides, you're getting a bit big for that now, aren't you?"

"Thank you, Mummy." Lu's voice comes out as a whisper because her throat has closed up. She tries to hold back her tears of disappointment. Going to the fete no longer appeals. Everyone will see the dress and think Second Hand Rose. They won't remember Ally's dress had blue and white smocking.

A Significant Other

Larissa Hikel

The dress reminds me of a street construction pylon. Hot orange. Screaming, florescent orange. If you conduct a Google search, you will not find this dress. I have not seen bright traffic-cone-orange tulle before or since.

A tight, strapless bodice features vertical rows of sliver sequins, while the waist is embellished with an elaborate finishing touch: a matching pylon-colored flower painstakingly edged in still more silver sequins. The flower, that resembles a huge lily, comes complete with a delicate rhinestone-tipped pistil.

The detail is breathtaking.

This dress is enormous.

The skirt is voluminous.

Should the skirt not consist of ultra-soft tulle, you would be unable to clear a standard doorway once safely inside the gown. Luckily, it could be smushed a little to allow the wearer to pass, after which it would certainly spring easily back to its original, incredible size and shape.

The embellished bodice twinkles from the hanger. The sequins flash defiantly each time a careless hand pulls at the gown and twists it to get a better look.

It's hot, neon orange (did I mention that?) with a tinge of blue fire. It screams from the circular rack of prom dresses in all of its $675.00 glory.

No one will ever buy this dress.

The bridal/formal wear shop is on the east side of town, so far east that it's the west side of the next town over. The street is pot-holed and rumbling and is served by a sad bus loop where I've yet to see a bus stop, let alone a waiting passenger.

Every day when I put the folding sign out onto what's left of the sidewalk, I'm honked or wooed at from passing trucks. I found this unnerving at first, but it soon became part of the routine. If I knew what was good for me, I would wave at the passing trucks in hopes that one would pull over. But I let these opportunities slip by, and obviously this is why I am still single.

It is dogma in this job that your wedding day, or—to a slightly lesser extent—your prom is the most important day of your life. Should you not be preparing for either of these, your life is worth nothing. I suppose you could still be waiting for the most important part of your life, which, incidentally, requires an invitation from someone else.

The shop is owned by Matthew.

He is of Korean descent. His wife pretends she speaks no English.

Matthew is spry, wily, inappropriate, and blames his wife when he doesn't want to do something or is in trouble for doing something.

One of his finest moments was inquiring of a shy teenager whether she was currently having her period in an attempt sell her a gown that would not be too tight later in the month. If this ploy were unsuccessful, he could then charge for alterations if the gown still did not fit later.

He practices several of these hustles. Another is selling "scarves" as an add-on to a dress. The scarves that come with the gowns are made of the excess fabric that remained after manufacturing. They arrive in the plastic bag containing the dress with love from the factory overseas. They're usually just a rectangle of fabric with a hem or a bit of embroidery that elevates the cloth from "remnant" to "wrap."

When a customer trying on a gown looks like they are going to bite, you seize the moment and produce a "scarf," awkwardly swaddling the customer in while convincing them it is imperative that this extra (which, strictly speaking, is just a remnant) be purchased for an additional $30. (Or maybe $20, or $50, depending on how you gauge your chances.)

There is a storeroom full of them in the shop. Among tall satin stacks of cream, oyster, white, and mother of pearl sits one lonely orange tulle scrap from the bottom of the pylon gown. It sits quietly on the shelf, where it wants to scream. It is a witness to this shady practice that keeps innocent fabric scraps on the shelf when they could be living their best lives. No one should charge for them; they have already been paid for.

Out on the sales floor, ambitious mothers insist that their event-attending young ladies try the orange dress. Just for fun. But there is nothing fun about a dress whose color casts a neon shadow onto fresh peach complexions, suddenly making them look ill.

One day, a spectacular blonde girl, 6 feet tall and with an angular face like a cut diamond, dons the dress. She resembles a wooden piece of furniture draped in a pylon-colored plastic sheet, like a table set for a construction-worker-themed child's birthday party. Her beauty is no match for the personality of the dress, which reduces her to an object of pity that one would cover with paper plates and a centerpiece and try to forget about.

She is only the latest to fall.

I am incredulous when another young woman chooses to try on the pylon. She is an opera singer with skin the color of crème brûlée. She has a head of big, shining mahogany curls. Once she has the pylon on, it is immediately clear to me that no one will ever wear this dress except for her.

Wherever she floats, the dress goes willingly. When she belts out a note of happiness, the sequins sparkle in approval.

Her face appears lit from within. If it's even possible, she is prettier than before. The dress, brighter than ever, gives her the look of a coral reef glistening underwater, or of a starfish, or of a crab nebula I've seen in photos of space. She is florescent fire opal, an Oregon silverspot butterfly.

It is a match made in heaven. This is clearly the most important day in the dress's life. I suspect the young woman may feel similarly.

Not a single glistening eyelash bats at the price tag.

This is the moment that the salesperson (me) will produce, as if by coincidence, a matching scarf! I drape it lovingly across the buyer's shoulders and silkily suggest that the additional $10 (or $15, if it's embroidered) is a wise investment, envisioning her getting cold and requiring twenty inches of tulle for additional warmth in a cocktail situation.

I hold the hot orange scrap of tulle that had come bagged with the dress up against my face in the dressing room mirror and shudder at how it makes my skin look like leftover meatloaf sans gravy. Back on the sales floor, I drape it across the opera singer's shoulders and the tulle comes to life, swirling lovingly around her neck and gracefully sweeping toward the floor in an elegant wisp.

"That's a difficult dress," I try.

The singer looks at me with polite interest but remains silent. It's true that on this particular subject there may be nothing to say. It is evident that I'm mistaken, that I've stated a falsehood. This dress isn't difficult. It is perfect.

I don't bother suggesting a tiara or offer to sew in foam bra cups in my clumsy way. I save everyone the trouble and proceed to asking if the lady desires a garment bag ($5). I am unable to deliver the scarf spiel. Instead, I include it—neatly folded—in the garment bag, without comment, and without charge.

THE WEDDING DRESS

Evelyn Forest

He loves her and she loves him. They are the most loving couple that ever lived, and handsome too. He holds her in his arms and says, "Tell me how much you love me."

Inside the cage of his arms, Evelyn tells him what he wants to hear, as if they are the only people in the world, as if their love is rare and precious. She tells him again that she loves him, but notices that the words become less true with each telling. The afternoon sun falls across the bed and lights upon her nakedness without reaching him.

She knows that when he says he loves her he means that she belongs to him. She knows that he's afraid of losing her. She can't forget what he said the time she tried to leave. She can't forget the gun.

"Let's get married," he says to her now, squeezing her. "Let's have a really big wedding."

The wedding takes place the same year as Charles and Diana's. After Diana, it is almost impossible to imagine a wedding dress that doesn't unfold like a flower when climbing out of a carriage. A dress with an enormous full skirt and giant puffball sleeves, trailing acres of crushed ivory silk taffeta, and the longest train in living memory. It is the ninth wonder of the world, a dress of such romance it could only belong in fairy tales. As Evelyn approaches her own wedding, a sense of unreality sets in that she would never describe as fairy-tale-like. It is more gothic, like being buried alive, or being forced to dig her own grave. She is trapped in a story she no longer believes in but can't rewrite.

Her friend Katie takes her to look at dresses, and nearly all of them are Diana dresses. She tries one on. It rustles as she lifts it over her head, and she fights to find the arm holes inside a tent of muted light. The pleasure she would normally take in the newness of the cloth is overshadowed by self-consciousness. How could she forget to wear good underwear for a shopping trip?

Evelyn gently shakes the folds down around her. Turning her chin over her left shoulder, she watches Katie close the zip, encasing her. They both look in the mirror as Katie smiles encouragement.

"Much cheaper to make one," Katie whispers. "Could you?"

Evelyn smiles and nods, because she could.

Katie pays for it all, an early wedding gift: yards and yards of creamy satin; luminous taffeta; chiffon; a reel of matching Silko mercerized cotton; an eight inch zipper; three pearl buttons; Simplicity pattern #3762.

The satin is heavy and cool when Evelyn lays it out. Holding each corner, she flicks her wrists and ripples it flat on the table. The satin lands in elegant folds, and she smooths the surface flat with her palms, straightening the edges. She pins on the pattern pieces, then checks and double checks until she finally cuts. Her scissors bite into the cloth and traverse the table, the cloth peeling away in the wake. She stacks the cut-out pieces like tissue paper sandwiches, leaving behind strange shapes that cling to the remnant in tails and scoops.

She had bought a second-hand sewing machine while still in high school, a solid, reliable Bernina with a knee-operated accelerator. Now she winds the bobbin, threads the top needle, then tests the tension on a scrap of satin. Adjusting her chair, she settles in and begins to join, stitch and sew. She thinks about the dress and the cloth, and what Katie said about choices.

As the machine ploughs through billowing cloth, she thinks about her little boy, their son. She thinks about her sister who will be her bridesmaid. With knee pressed to the accelerator and hands guiding, holding, and supporting, she thinks about her parents who are paying for the wedding. She keeps the trail of stitches parallel to the shaggy edge, like writing a sentence. She thinks about the wedding she once imagined for herself, then shifts her attention back to the dress and the seam and the pins. She tries not to prick her finger and bloody the fabric. Her eye is on the needle piercing the cloth with its sharp point. She thinks about the man she's going to marry and looks up for one wrong moment and sews her own finger to the dress.

When the wedding is over, she doesn't know what to do with the dress. She knows that other brides preserve their dresses for their future daughters in layers of tissue paper inside big flat boxes. Her own mother kept hers in a plastic bag in a drawer until it was lost in a house fire. But Evelyn has come to hate her dress.

For years after the marriage ends, she still carts the dress around, unwilling to give up on all that had been gifted to her, and all her work. Then a day arrives when she stuffs it through the after-hours slot at the second-hand shop downtown. She struggles to push it through, and has a moment of panic, fearing that someone will see her. She wants to erase not only her doomed wedding, but also the froth of pretense she constructed with her own hands.

Bizarrely, the dress later returns to her in a story told by an acquaintance who volunteers at that shop. He regularly regales people with stories of the weird and fascinating stuff he comes across, and her dress has made it into his canon. At the dinner they're attending, he mocks it with humiliating accuracy, heaping scorn on the maker and the bride who wore it, a deluded woman mimicking a deluded princess. He chortles at how fantastically wrong it was.

Evelyn has to leave the room, fearing her face will betray her, but is amazed that other people hate the dress as much as she does.

It Matches Your Eyes

Madeleine McDonald

"We've time to do one more drawer before I collect Oliver from school." Kate scoops my neatly folded scarves and gloves into a pile on the bed. My daughter, I regret to say, is an incurable bossy-boots. On the excuse that her dad and I are downsizing, she has chivvied me into giving away half my wardrobe. Bulging plastic bags by the bedroom door testify to her efficiency.

"This can go." She throws a fringed scarf onto the rags pile.

I retrieve it.

"Mum, why do you want to keep that one? It's not you. It looks hippy-ish." Kate has never minced her words.

"It's a pretty color. It goes with a lot of my things."

"I've never seen you wear it." She has already lost interest and is examining a woolen beret for moth holes.

I discipline myself not to react, nor to stroke the scarf. It is returned to the drawer where it has lived since my marriage thirty-six years ago.

Kate is right. The scarf does look hippy-ish. For an entire year I had worn it, paired with blue flared trousers and a cream top woven through with gold Lurex thread. Few photos from that year have survived, and none show me with Alexander.

My daughter has yet to learn that some wounds can be too deep to ever heal.

○ ♡ ○

It was one of those days when England enjoys unexpected sun, putting everyone in a good mood. Xander and I were taking a shortcut through the market stalls on our way to the university when, without warning, he pulled a patterned scarf from a display rack and looped it round my neck. "There! It matches your eyes. I can never make up my mind whether they're blue or grey."

I was surprised, and secretly delighted, for Xander was not the kind of person to pay idle compliments. I took to wearing it every day.

A year later, I wore that scarf to say goodbye. There was still a chill in the air as we sat on a bench by the river and watched a toddler feeding bread to the ducks, shrieking with delight when one with a clutch of ducklings paddled over. His mother's arm pulled him back when he strayed too near the edge. Xander's arm lay loosely around my shoulders until I drew away and faced him. My nails dug into my clenched palms. Did he already know what I had to say? Probably yes, at some deep, unacknowledged level. Back then, our minds were so in tune, as if we had a private language of things unsaid.

"I'm not coming to Australia," I blurted out.

Xander had come up with the plan for us to travel around Australia on a working visa, a few months of adventure before we both applied for proper jobs. I knew his degree in geology would open doors Down Under but was not so sure about my qualifications. A BA in English literature seemed irrelevant.

Xander had waved away my doubts. "You can do waitressing or something. I want to see the outback. I know a guy who can get me sheep-shearing jobs. He showed me the basics when he worked on my uncle's farm last summer. I'll make enough money for the two of us for a while, then we'll go north to Darwin. You can find work there."

When he first said that, I had laughed. "You? Shearing sheep?"

He lunged and flipped me on the sofa and made buzzing sounds as he mimicked removing a heavy fleece. Although I wriggled, there was strength in his scrawny frame. The mock shearing turned into a tickling session, but the question of what jobs I could find while he did the jackaroo bit remained unresolved. My annoyance at his cavalier attitude festered in silence.

Later that morning, by the river, Xander went straight to the point. "It's not just Australia, is it?" I dropped my gaze before his accusing stare.

"No. Last weekend, when I went to see my parents, I... I met Richard again."

"Your old boyfriend? I thought he was history."

"So did I. I can't explain. It just happened. Seeing him again, we felt right together." By now I was crying, and the woman with the toddler moved away, giving us privacy.

I could not bear the hurt in his eyes.

"For one thing, Xander, you're clever, really clever, and I'm not."

He was pacing round, picking up pebbles and flinging them in the water. "What's that got to do with it?"

"Everything. You've got a mind like a firecracker, fizzing off in all directions. I could never keep up with you intellectually. I would always be two steps behind. That's no basis for a life together."

I detected acknowledgement in his eyes. Back then, Xander was a rare example of a working-class boy who had made it to university. He was not just good, he was outstanding. I once saw him read a textbook on probability theory to 'relax his mind' the night before an important examination. However, being an outstanding scholar did not make him popular. Like all self-taught people, he had no patience with facile thinking.

When he argued that a working visa lasted ten months and not a lifetime, I plunged on. I so badly wanted him to understand. "I can make a life with Richard. What I'm saying is he won't challenge me or drag me off on wild adventures. I'm a homebody at heart, Xander. You can't change me."

We went back to his room and made wordless love with a ferocity I never thought possible, the smell of his skin blotting out all loss and longing. One more day, one more hour. When he bivouacked under the Southern Cross, I wanted him to remember me.

Then it was time for me to leave.

Xander never wrote. Neither did I. Some wounds go too deep to heal. People easily disappeared off the radar before the Internet or Facebook. Ten years after we'd graduated, I met one of his friends at a university reunion. "Xan? Last I heard, he was in Papua New Guinea. He said the locals didn't like that mining company, but I'd back old Xan against the cannibals any day." On that insensitive remark, he moved away.

I went to the toilet and sat in a cubicle until my breathing returned to normal. I buried my face in the blue-grey scarf, which I had worn in case he came. I had left Richard at home, looking after the little ones, bless him. It was foolish to think Xander was any more lost to me now—somewhere in the Papuan jungle—than he had been ten years before.

I, too, would back Xander against cannibals, fire, floods or earthquakes, as well as articulate, educated protesters defending their ancestral land rights in the law courts. There was a ruthless streak in him that allied with his impatience and lack of compassion. In a previous age, he might well have been a privateer, growing rich on his share of plunder on the high seas and relying solely on his wits to keep himself out of trouble back home.

Xander took the road less travelled. I married Richard and was pregnant within the year. The scarf came with me into our new home, a hidden reminder of the day I tore my soul in half.

Sometimes, when I glimpsed myself in the mirror wearing the scarf, the sticking plaster of my self-deceit would rip open. Xander, the other half of myself, stood between me and my reflection, bareheaded in the spring sunshine, carelessly looping a purchase from the market stall round my neck. In those moments, the raw hurt was unbearable.

I always rationalized my feelings. Yes, what Xander and I had had together was beautiful and unique, inside our university bubble. There was nothing wrong in cherishing his memory—although Richard must never guess.

After a while, it was enough to know the scarf was somewhere under the pile in my drawer. Life was tough, and I needed its presence to convince myself I had made the right choice. When the children were small and our mortgage rate rose to 15%, Richard and I required financial help from both sets of parents. We all slept in one room in winter to save on heating bills. Richard, bless him, did overtime to earn extra money, but was poor company in the evenings. He was usually asleep by 9 o'clock, a deep and snoring sleep of exhaustion.

Richard's snoring became my comfort blanket, a reminder that he and I had followed the safe and steadfast path. Knowing that somewhere under the Southern Cross Xander followed his own intrepid track, I wished him well. He would not forget me. He could not.

Now, here we are, thirty-six years later. I linger in the bedroom with a cup of tea on the pretense of reorganizing my much-depleted wardrobe.

I hear Kate calling from the kitchen where she is throwing out pots and pans. She says something about the slow cooker. "If you want it, take it," I shout. I lack the energy to counter her ruthless decluttering.

Then Oliver bounces in and takes a flying leap onto the bed. Richard follows at a more sedate pace.

"Grandma, Grandma, we're going to make a scarecrow to put in the garden and look after the old house when you and Granddad move. Mum says I can use some of your old clothes."

With the irrepressible determination of an eight-year-old he is already untying one of the plastic bags,

"Wait, Oliver, let me." I find the right bag and retrieve one of Richard's office shirts. "Do you want a tie as well? Here."

Oliver pouts. "I don't want him to have a tie. I want to make a Batman scarecrow."

"That's going to be difficult." After some discussion, Granddad and I persuade him to dress the scarecrow as a pirate. Between us we spread various items of clothing on the bed, undoing most of Kate's work.

Finding no suitable belts, I pull the blue-grey scarf from its hiding place. "Here, take this to knot around his waist." Oliver approves.

The juggernaut of life, in the person of my beloved grandson, piles the repurposed scarf on top of his other booty and scampers away to start work.

I no longer need the tangible caress of soft blue-grey cotton after all these years. It will be enough to know that, somewhere under the Southern Cross, the other half of my soul remembers me.

Contributors

Farah Ahamed's short stories and essays have been published in *Ploughshares, The Mechanics' Institute Review, The Massachusetts Review* amongst others, and nominated for the Pushcart and Caine prizes. In 2021, Pan Macmillan will publish her non-fiction anthology on menstruation experiences in South Asia. She is currently working on a collection of short stories and a novel. You can read more of her work here: farahahamed.com

Lindsay Bamfield has had a number of short stories and flash fiction pieces published online and in anthologies, including *Mslexia, Reflex Fiction* and *Flash Flood Journal.*

Gabriella Brand's short stories, poems and essays have appeared in over fifty literary magazines, including *Aji, Rockvale Review, Room, The First Line, StepAway,* and several anthologies. One of her short stories was nominated for a Pushcart Prize. Gabriella divides her time between Connecticut, where she teaches foreign languages, and the Eastern Townships of Quebec, where she volunteers with refugees, hikes like a demon, and paddles her own canoe. Her website is gabriellabrand.net.

Susan Carey lives in Amsterdam where she teaches English as a second language and writes stories in between the more important jobs of dog-walking and dreaming of worldwide renown. She has had short stories and flash fiction published and performed by, amongst others, *Mslexia, Liars' League, Stringybark Publishing, Writers Abroad, Reflex Fiction, Flash Flood Journal* and *Casket of Fictional Delights*. In 2020 she published her story collection, *Healer*. Available on Amazon.

Brian Centrone is a writer, editor, and fashion historian specializing in menswear and pop culture. He is the editor of *Salon Style: Fiction, Poetry & Art*, as well as the co-editor of *Southern Gothic: New Tales of the South*. His fashion research has appeared in *Threads* magazine, the *FIDM Museum Blog*, the *FIT Fashion History Timeline*, and the *Bloomsbury Encyclopedia of Film and Television Costume Design* (forthcoming). He is the author of the novel *An Ordinary Boy* and two short story collections, *I Voted for Biddy Schumacher: Mismatched Tales from the Mind of Brian Centrone* and *Erotica*.

Evelyn Forest completed the manuscript of her first novel with clothes and appearances as a central theme in 2019. She has a Ph.D in social aspects of dress, and has worked for years in various roles at the University of Otago in New Zealand, publishing academic work on school uniforms, red shoes and boudoir caps, among other less interesting things. She is also a dressmaker of moderate skill.

Larissa Hikel is a writer, actor and photographer with a lot of weird ideas. She alternates between sleepless nights of productivity and doing nothing for weeks at a time. Her first writing gig was providing the fortunes for the inside of cookies given away at a birthday party. She still wonders about those kids and whether they decided to take the free advice. In between recovering from rejection letters, she enjoys eavesdropping, libraries, and making clothes. Her writing has been published in *Nature's Healing Spirit: Real Life Stories to Nurture the Soul* and performed onstage in Sarasvati Productions annual Bake-Off.

Blake Jessop is a Canadian author of sci-fi, fantasy and horror stories with a master's degree in creative writing from the University of Adelaide. You can read more of his punk rock speculative fiction in the second issue of *DreamForge Magazine*, or follow him on Twitter @everydayjisei.

Gerri Leen lives in Northern Virginia and originally hails from Seattle. In addition to being an avid reader, she's passionate about horse racing, tea, ASMR vids, and creating weird tacos. She has work appearing in *Nature, Escape Pod, Daily Science Fiction, Cast of Wonders,* and others. She's edited several anthologies for independent presses, is finishing some longer projects, and is a member of SFWA and HWA. See more at http://www.gerrileen. com.

Cheney Luttich teaches writing at a local community college. In her free time, she writes all sorts of things and devours anything related to historical clothing. She currently lives in Omaha, Nebraska, with her husband and two daughters.

Madeleine McDonald lives on the chilly east coast of England where the cliffs crumble into the sea. She finds inspiration walking on the beach before the world wakes up. Her third romance novel, *A Shackled Inheritance,* is available from Amazon.

P.J. Schaefer earned her Ph.D. in American literature at Fordham University, New York. In addition to a host of academic publications, she has also published long and short mainstream fiction and nonfiction. Her works have appeared in such publications as *Troika; Dogsongs; Reader's Break; Elements; Ink; Poor Katie's Almanac; Behind the Yellow Wallpaper: New Tales of Madness; First Came Fear: New Tales of Horror; Salon Style: Fiction, Poetry, & Art; Offshore: Northeast Boating; Boston Parents' Paper; Big Apple Parent; Children's Writer; Family.*

Stephen Tornero is a textile artist and art educator. He teaches Fashion Design and Visual Art to 7th and 8th graders while pursuing his own weaving practice and showing work at galleries and museums. Stephen's interest in fashion began at age 8 when he was allowed to pick out his own clothes at the store for the first time. He understands the psychological and spiritual effects that fashion can have on himself and his very trendy students. He currently lives and works in Ohio and has a M.A. in Art Education from Kent State University.

Linda Welters is a professor in the Textiles, Fashion Merchandising and Design Department at the University of Rhode Island. She teaches the history of fashion. Her most recent book is *Fashion History: A Global View* (Bloomsbury 2018) co-authored with Abby Lillethun. Currently she is at work on the third edition of *The Fashion Reader*, co-edited with Abby Lillethun and *Fashioning America*, co-authored with Patricia Cunningham.

Also available from NLSP

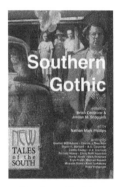

Southern Gothic:
New Tales of the South
edited by Brian Centrone and
Jordan M. Scoggins

Behind the Yellow Wallpaper:
New Tales of Madness
edited by Rose Yndigoyen

Startling Sci-Fi:
New Tales of the Beyond
edited by Casey Ellis

First Came Fear:
New Tales of Horror
edited by Casey Ellis

Salon Style:
Fiction, Poetry & Art
edited by Brian Centrone

I Voted for
Biddy Schumacher:
Mismatched Tales from the Mind
of Brian Centrone

newlitsalonpress.com

CPSIA information can be obtained
at www.ICGtesting.com
Printed in the USA
BVHW050922130421
604821BV00003B/335

9 780997 264937